EATING STARS

ANGEL MARTINEZ

EDITED BY
JAYMI E

BLURB_

The escape pods fall to Earth one by one over the course of weeks, a mysterious and diverse alien diaspora, each pod containing a different alien race and leaving the world's governments scrambling to deal with this unexpected immigration. Serge Kosygin, still grieving and isolated after his husband's death, watches events with gray disinterest until one day he witnesses a pod crash for himself while driving home. Two of the alien visitors have died, but one survives, badly injured, and Serge is determined that if this alien is also going to die, it won't be under the harsh lights of a government facility.

Devastated by the loss of his life mates in their desperate effort to reach safety, the knowledge that Een is the last Aalana in this sector of the galaxy only compounds his sorrow. He wakes in an alien dwelling under the care of one of the native dominant builder species, a being who appears to share nothing with Een besides a bipedal structure. Slowly, with the help of his patient and kind host, he discovers they are more similar than he imagined as they share harmonies and his host assists him with language acquisition.

Their tentative first contact soon evolves into a deepening friendship, a balm for two grief-weary souls. They'll need each other and their growing bond for the troubles lurking just ahead.

PUBLISHER'S NOTE_

Eating Stars was previously published as part of Meteor *Strike: Serge & Een* as a novelette. It has undergone extensive rewrites and edits with over 10,000 words of new content added.

There is also an added glossary at the back for your reference.

For C.S. Friedman and C.J. Cherryh who showed me that, yes, an Earthbound dirt-sucker could think in alien.

CONTENTS

TRADEMARK ACKNOWLEDGEMENTS_

Silly String: SILLY STRING
     Products
Sno-Cat: Tucker Sno-Cat
     Corporation
Star Trek: Paramount Pictures
     Corporation
X-Files: 20th Century Fox

Wᴇɴ ᴛʜᴇ ɢʀᴀʏ sʜɪᴘs ʜᴀᴅ ꜰɪʀsᴛ ᴀᴘᴘᴇᴀʀᴇᴅ ᴀᴛ the outer rim, Aalana system stations attempted contact and assumed that the lack of response was due to a need to acquire language first. They had established contact with several other spacefaring people by that time, and had experienced hesitance before, waiting to speak with the Aalana until they could do so and be understood.

The ships' continued silence worried Een as he tracked them from his listening post with growing concern.

"Laiin?" he sang over to where she worked at her data station. "Have you calculated their trajectories?"

"I do so now." Her notes conveyed shared concern, but her hands never faltered over her numbers. "Message home, Een. Query status. Aal, inform the director."

Ships from first contact people usually approached by degrees, but these ships, sleek and fast, hurtled through the system, arrowing toward the Aalana homeworld with dreadful purpose. Een and his mates, Laiin and Aal, had been working as deep-space listeners on one of the far-orbiting stations closest to the system's edge for several revolutions and had never seen anything like this.

The director gathered all of the station employees into the listening station's pod where they waited together, *lim* waving, nearly everyone humming in concern. The hours between query and answer were agonizing and Een nestled between his mates, shivering. They huddled closer when the horrifying message finally reached them, broken and desperate.

All... communication failed. Beams... widespread destruction... all cities... silent.... millions dead. They slaughter... careless abandon... medical... crèches... all gone. We are the last. All are gone. Our pleas... no mindfulness... only death.

The director hesitated only a moment, her *faiina* all standing up in sharp, shocked points. Then she began to sing in a strong, martial tone and point to her people. "Go, Check the jumpship. Take all we can in supplies. Send beacons out with this message to every deep-space Aalana ship we have on file, every other in-system station. Send the message from home and add to it, *Flee. Scatter. Take your mates and your offspring and run. We must survive.*"

Almost the last to leave, Een and his station colleagues barely escaped in their single jump ship as the gray war vessels began to sweep the system for remaining Aalana. From the viewports they watched, clinging together as the hostile ships fired upon the poor little station that had been their home. They could only watch in helpless horror as the station exploded in a bright, single flare.

They ran silent, unwilling to give the gray ships transmissions to trace, songs their scattered people might feel compelled to answer and thus betray their own locations as well. No *why* emerged in their time of flight, no reason an alien race would wish to annihilate a peaceful people. While some of the youngest Aalana speculated and agonized over motives and how the disaster might have been averted, most of them knew there could be no adequate reason, no justification for genocide.

Rumors and whispers led them to Sanctuary, an ingenious, multispecies station populated mainly by others who had fled the invaders, each from their own doomed home planets. Hollowed out asteroids connected in strings and clusters by force fields served as habitats and common spaces, brimming with races both familiar and new to the Aalana refugees.

The gray ships would come. No one doubted that eventuality. The enemy would track their prey. The various races combined their knowledge and technologies in a two-pronged effort: first, find a planet in a far-flung arm of the galaxy on which to make a stand and second, invent a way to allow the entire station to make the jump. Many of the jump ships had arrived damaged and Sanctuary no longer had a fleet large enough to accommodate all the refugees.

Too soon, outlier scouts sent the alarm. The gray ships were coming. The new field emitter configuration wasn't ready, but they had no time. With the enemy closing on them, they were forced to make the jump, damaging the field generator and the emitter array. In the catastrophic field generator failure, the explosion had destroyed all the central habitats and sent the surviving asteroids hurtling away from each other. Those who remained set course in a last, harried attempt to reach the target planet. From all the grief-stricken, frightened messages back and forth, Een's pod had been the only Aalana vessel remaining after the generator explosion.

In their desperate flight here, how many species had been lost? How many songs had died?

The scattered pods limped toward the third planet from this system's star on widely spaced trajectories. It would take days upon days for all of the pods to reach their goal and Een's would be among the last to arrive. By then, perhaps, they would know if the people of this planet had reacted with more curiosity than hostility to their landing. They had no viable choices remaining. These alien beings were their last and only hope.

———

SERGE DISMISSED the first newscast he saw as another *War of the Worlds* hoax. Interesting story, but just a story. He'd also had a few beers, so he didn't think about verifying with another news source, just changed the channel to a documentary about an abandoned fortress and fell asleep on the couch.

He'd been doing that a lot lately—wandering aimlessly from room to room all day and ending up with beer for dinner in front of the TV. Not healthy by a long shot. He knew it and was trying to cut back on just being...aimless. He did have to get into town soon. Man couldn't live by beer alone. With other things weighing down his mind, he'd forgotten about the pod landing.

Until the next night, when three more landed. Finally, he thought to check and the story repeated on every news station. Pods. From space. Now that this strange development had penetrated the thick fog of his life, Serge watched with something like curiosity, then growing concern.

It didn't take long for the world to figure out the pods weren't an invasion. They were refugees from some disaster and each pod so far had contained a different kind of alien. The knee-high, round furred ones who seemed to be communicating successfully with the Norwegians. The millipede sort of ones who weren't doing as well with the Canadians. The manta ones in their water hover-things who had landed in the US...

The news only showed the same thirty-second footage of them, nothing after initial contact, and Serge watched closely, suspicions growing, as more pods came down across the states over the next few days. Government officials would come on to acknowledge each landing and to say that the aliens were receiving all the help they needed, but none of the alien people appeared in front of the cameras again.

The part of him that could still care enough to worry conjured up secret federal facilities with cold, unfeeling scientists and terrible experiments. The country's track record with refugee treatment wasn't the best, after all, and the way the aliens vanished was nothing short of sinister. But really, what could he do? It wasn't any of his business and he wasn't some action hero to go swooping in and rescuing anyone from unethical labs.

Nope. Better to see what was still in the cupboard and try to figure out if he needed to stock up on anything before the next snow moved in.

CHAPTER ONE

Smoke rose from the damaged pod. Difficult to say how much, since it was obscured by the windswept snow. This was supposed to be a mild season in this hemisphere. The instruments had only given them general data, not enough to take elevation and local weather patterns into account.

"Field release," Een whispered.

A last sliver of hope insisted that the AI functions might have survived the crash. No response. He fumbled with the manual release, fingers clumsy and swollen, difficult to maneuver with all his *faiina* still upright in hard spikes from fear and pain.

Perhaps his containment field failed as well, since it shut down suddenly, leaving him free to crawl from his command bowl out of the ruined pod. Grief jostled with frustration in his jumbled thoughts. *Almost.* They had been so close. On the outer rim of the escaping fleet, their small asteroid pod had escaped the worst of the damage from the failure of the fleet's field generators. Even so, they suffered localized instrument failures and the loss of outbound communications. They could only listen in horror as other pod crews cried out for assistance, desperate emergency calls in a dozen languages cut off mid-word, lives suddenly extinguished that the AI registered only as blank space in the data.

Dragging his burned and uncooperative body one-armed, he reached Aal. Once shining silver eyes stared sightless, flat and dark, at an alien sky. Forcibly ejected when the pod crashed, Aal's neck had snapped. Perhaps it was kinder that way. Laiin's remains lay farther on, twisted, burned, no remnant now of that quick, bright laugh, the graceful shadow dancer. They had been all Een had left, the last of his home—this world had chosen cruelty over mercy and taken them.

So close, they had come so close to safety.

The outer hull had burned off on entry, following its design, most likely leaving a bright trail of fire in its wake as they plummeted into the gravity well. They had held on, singing the patterns, joyful that they had reached sanctuary. Then on approach, the EM fields failed, transforming what should have been a hard landing into a catastrophic crash.

Somewhere out in the vast bowl of stars, there might be more Aalana. But here, beneath this chill sky, gray as death, he was the last. *I welcome you, Light-Singer. Gather me into your arms.*

But death turned her back and refused his embrace, leaving him bereft and in agony in this terrible, barren place.

———

THIS IS A STUPID IDEA. The truck tires skidded again, almost taking Serge off the road this time. *Really stupid.*

Late spring snow hadn't been in the damn forecast yet. Though that happened this time of year, turning the thaw from the previous week into ice sheets lurking under the soft powder. Not for the first time, he cussed up enough heat to melt all the snow between Pittsburgh and Buffalo as he fought the wheel and thought about turning back for home. It had to be coming up soon, though. He'd tracked the path. He'd *seen* it hit. Not *land* as he'd been watching some of the others do on the news channels over the past weeks, but hurtle down in a bright burst of orange and red.

If it was just a meteor, fine. He'd make a note of the location and call it in to the authorities. Get the astronomical team from University of Pittsburgh out here. But if it wasn't? If it was one of the inhabited pods touching down across the globe, he couldn't turn his back and say, *oh, well, not my problem.* Some poor sod might need help. A shifting glow painted the snow up ahead and only when he spotted the site did a thought hit him. Maybe there was so much hush-hush going on about the nature of the aliens landing because some of them weren't peaceful sorts. Maybe this was Serge being the idiot at the start of a horror movie, the one who gets killed in the first five minutes.

Yeah, and if you turn back now, Josh is gonna... Serge pulled his thoughts up short. Josh wasn't going to say anything when he got home. He wasn't coming home, not that night or the next. No more coming home.

The back tires slipped again and Serge eased the

wheel over to compensate. Not the time to wallow. He had to concentrate on the road or this trip would end up killing him. When he could see the flames jumping and skittering in the wind, he pulled onto the shoulder, grabbed the flashlight from under the seat, and jumped out. The snow wasn't deep, but the footing was treacherous, so he stepped carefully, edging out into the field where the meteor or craft had landed.

"Mother of God," he breathed out as his eyes adjusted. His brain lagged a few seconds behind as he took in the tragic scene scattered across the snow.

It had been a craft of some sort, an oblong shape resembling a seedpod, if he could extrapolate from what remained. Three occupants had been ejected from the craft. If there were more, those poor bastards were trapped in the firestorm devouring the vehicle. There was no help for them.

The figure closest to him was twisted into an agonized fetal position, most of its clothing burned away, the body underneath black with char. The close-fitting helmet, he assumed it was a helmet and not the being's head, was cracked and the face shield had melted. Serge couldn't bring himself to look any closer. He trudged on to the other two, lying close together, one on its back and the other with a hand on the supine being's chest, as if trying to offer comfort before they died. He didn't know them, didn't even know what they were, but still the backs of his eyes stung at that last moment of...devotion, love, loyalty? Just as sad, no matter what the motivation.

He was going to have to call the police and have them come up here. Do whatever they did in these situations. But his feet kept moving forward instead of returning to the truck. Damn snow kept blowing around too much. He had to make sure, but the one with the hand placed so tenderly... Serge was sure he'd seen that one move. *Yes.* The helmeted head lifted. A crooning note drifted to him through the snow, a sound so heart-wrenchingly sad, Serge teared up again.

"You're still alive, you poor bugger," Serge murmured. Police? Ambulance? Shouldn't he get this visitor some help? Problem was, he questioned what was really happening to the refugees who'd managed to land here. Were the world's governments really welcoming them or were they isolating them for "study," holding them captive and traumatizing them in the name of either science or global security?

What would Josh have done? Probably held up his middle finger and waved it at the authorities in one way or another. *Think, Kosygin. You don't have much medical training. You don't even have supplies to start an IV.* Of course, the alien might not have veins. An IV might kill him. In that regard, he wasn't any worse as a caretaker than hospital staff would be. If this was a new species, and every landed craft so far had been different, they'd all be starting from scratch on the physiology and anatomy front.

He shouldn't get involved. Why should he even care? It had nothing to do with him.

And right there, that stopped him short. When had it gotten so bad that he didn't care? He'd withdrawn from the world, from his job and his friends, but that didn't mean he'd drive by a person stranded and injured at the side of the road, did it? Had he changed that much?

To leave an alien visitor to the authorities when

they were helpless, unable to speak for themself, to defend themself if necessary—it felt horribly wrong.

His feet moved, his body convinced of his decision before he'd been able to make one, the night took on a strange, dreamlike quality as he rolled the survivor over and lifted the unresponsive body into his arms. Once Serge had his passenger settled and covered in blankets from the back seat, he called in the crash and reported two bodies, saying he couldn't wait any longer out in the storm if he expected to get home in one piece.

His passenger's dirge or hymn or whatever the song was quieted to occasional murmurs of single notes and short phrases, the alien's head rolling with the truck's movements.

"Stay with me, buddy," Serge said as he took the last turn up the long hill to his house. "Don't die in my damn truck."

No reason at all for the location of death to make a bit of difference, but some part of Serge was determined that if his guest was in his last moments, the dying would be done in a warm, comfortable bed. The truck slipped more than once going up the hill, tires spinning in a desperate bid for traction. Finally, they reached the drive and Serge could shut off the engine and jog around to the passenger side. His impromptu guest was rangy, probably a good half foot taller than Serge, but couldn't have weighed more than the average twelve-year-old. *They* as opposed to *she* or *he* or another gender label entirely might not have been remotely correct. No way to tell. *They* would do until Serge knew better.

The two steps onto the porch nearly ended in disaster as Serge's foot slipped. *Should've salted when the snow started.* Then he had to juggle his passenger to his left arm, supported on one knee, while he dealt with the sticky screen door and got the front door unlocked. He needed to fix that and the whole front of the house needed painting.

So many things he'd been neglecting.

The guest room was an embarrassment too, used as storage the past several years. Serge used an elbow to flick the light switch, kicked boxes off the bed, and eased his alien guest onto the comforter. In the soft lamplight, Serge took a moment to see what he'd gotten himself into. Bipedal, bilateral symmetry, two arms, fingers, a head, all familiar things, at least. His guest didn't appear to have extra appendages like wings or a tail. So far, so good. Parts of the alien's coverall had burned and Serge leaned in closer to puzzle out fastenings to start peeling them out of the smoke-infused material.

There. A seam along the side came apart when pressed on either edge. Carefully, Serge started to fold the coverall back and it finally hit him that despite the human number of limbs, this being was entirely alien. The unburned dermal covering was...feathers? No, not quite, but that was the closest analogous covering Serge could come up with. Triangular points overlapping in a sort of scale arrangement, they were soft and, under lamplight at least, a pearlescent lavender. The hands had six digits—five fingers of nearly equal length and a thumb, all tipped with pale, smooth pads.

He tugged gently when he got to the burned shoulder, wincing when the damn coverall stuck and ripped off one of the feather-scales.

"Sorry...sorry. I'll be right back," Serge whispered and hurried to the kitchen for a sponge.

Wetting the material with the sponge on the underside as he lifted allowed him to remove the coverall bit by painstaking bit. The water didn't cause any more damage as far as Serge could tell, so one possible Earth hurdle down, at any rate. Burned feather-scales crumbled off in tiny showers of black ash as he progressed down the alien's side, leaving bare, pale skin underneath.

Once he'd worked the coverall down to his guest's waist, the burns laid bare weren't as bad as he'd thought. Pressure suit, flame retardant, whatever the nature of the alien material, it had offered more protection than seemed likely for such a thin barrier. Serge hauled ice out of the freezer chest and packed it around the burned arm and side. He bundled the rest of his visitor in heavy blankets from the closet since the unburned skin was frigid.

The helmet worried him, with its cracked faceplate and unfamiliar catches, but he managed to flip the right paddles and ease the bulbous thing off. When he set the helmet aside, the alienness only increased. Instead of hair, finger-thick fronds covered the alien's head, the strange twitching appendages a few shades of lavender darker than the bare skin of the face. The eyelids were rounder, though not much larger than human eyes. Two small nostrils were in roughly the usual place, but set flush as a seal's would be. Mouth and ears were both recognizable, but just different enough to be uncanny. Pulse...yes, there was a sluggish pulse, but Serge reminded himself that he had no idea what was normal, and respirations seemed unhindered, so at least Earth's oxygen level seemed to be compatible.

Niggles of guilt prodded at him again, the ones that said he should take the alien to the authorities and medical staff. This species hadn't been in any of the previous meteor landing news coverage, though. The medical staff wouldn't know any more than he did, and the stress of a hospital might kill the alien quicker. Horrible places. Better to let his visitor rest quietly overnight, wait for the storm to die down, and see how he was doing in the morning.

The hospital would be the last resort.

———

BOTH WARMTH and cold surrounded Een, so he must have been suffering hallucinations or possible neural damage. Whatever the cause of the strange temperature dysphoria, at least his location was quiet and relatively comfortable. He opened his eyes to darkness, unable to focus. The quality of sound as he shifted suggested that he was inside a structure of some sort, but that seemed unlikely.

Perhaps one of the native sentients had recovered him despite the atmospheric storm? If only there had been more data on the planet's dominant builder species. If one of them had scooped him up, he was perhaps as likely to be eaten as he was to be cared for, and if they had shut him inside without access to photon emissions, their intent would hardly matter.

He would die, perhaps the last of his kind. Without long-range communication at his fingertips, he had no way to know. While the Aalana had delighted in exploring the stars for centuries, they had been naïve, and their belief in a benevolent universe had proved deadly.

In his distress, calling for Laiin and Aal was instinctive, the whisper-trill of notes escaping him before he could stop them. His chest constricted as he reminded himself they weren't coming to hold him and tell him all was well. Never again. The loss of their warmth, their *voices* hurt far more than his burned side. The desire to wail for them welled inside until it nearly won, but his surroundings were uncertain, possibly unsafe. If he were a braver Aalana, he wouldn't worry about safety. What did it matter? Without his mates...

But light soon filtered into the room and Een's weary, frightened brain concluded that the structure wasn't entirely enclosed. It had been night. He could barely make out the shape of the alien across the room, presumably asleep in an awkward half-sitting posture. Certainly not immediately threatening and in the bits Een could recall from coming here, those strange hands had been gentle, the voice soft.

Een's body yearned toward the growing patch of light in the center of the room. Had the alien being known he would need it? Perhaps guessed at possibilities and in that alone rested enormous kindness. Pain accompanied each movement as Een slid from the sleeping platform and crawled toward the light. Pain would always live with him now and someday death would come. But not today.

Today, someone had offered what appeared to be a mindful act on his behalf and it would be wrong to waste it.

———

Serge jerked awake from an anxious dream in which Josh led him through shadowed corridors, urging him to hurry. Stairs had suddenly appeared under his feet. The risers crumbled as he fell.

Sunlight streamed through the open curtains of the guest room, which wasn't right. He always closed the curtains for extra insulation on cold nights. *Other things on my mind last night.* He stretched, turned to check on his guest, and choked on his next breath. The blankets lay twisted and bunched, the pillow tossed toward the wall, but the bed was empty. The alien could be anywhere. Belated alarm hammered through him. He'd assumed his rescued alien was peaceful, an oversight that might mean his death.

He turned his head slowly, scanning the room, heart pounding as his imagination supplied more and more grisly images of the alien lunging at him to rip him to shreds. No alien hunter lurked behind his chair or in the corners, though. Instead, a crumpled heap of lavender occupied the rectangle of sunlight in the middle of the carpet. Naked, curled up tight, the alien had claimed that spot and appeared to be trying to get as much of their body into the patch of light as possible. Forehead wrinkling in concern, Serge knelt beside the alien and touched one lavender shoulder. Strange. Even without any covers, the feather-scales were warm, far warmer than the previous evening. That was better, wasn't it?

Maybe. Or maybe it was this being's version of a fever.

"Hey." He leaned over and gave the alien a gentle shake. "Floor's probably not the best place to be."

The alien's eyelids flickered, blinking open to reveal uniformly silver eyes. The soft trill of notes sounded quizzical, maybe a disoriented question, but Serge had no idea what was being asked. Gently, he slid his arms under his patient, lifting them to take them back to the bed. The trill became a note of distress, or possibly alarm, as the alien stretched a shaking hand back toward the rectangle of sunlight.

"Um, okay?" Serge tried stepping back into the sunlight, and the unhappy notes ceased, the alien settling more calmly in his arms. When he stepped out of the direct light again, those silver eyes snapped open and the agitated notes began again.

He was working on guesses, but there did appear to be a need, or at least a desperate desire, for sunlight.

"Let's do this right, then."

Serge bundled the alien back in their blankets and carried them to the front room where the darkness ratcheted up the agitated notes from distress to dismay. He set his bundle on the floor, strode to the bay window, and flung open the curtains. Immediately, the alien reached for the larger rectangle of light, crooning softly and squirming out of the blankets until they lay sprawled in the sunlight, their eyes closing again, their notes quieting to occasional soft chimes.

"Better, huh?" Serge crouched beside them, making certain this was where they wanted to be. "Not what I'd pick after being burned like that, but okay."

He picked up the blankets and settled them over his guest. With a soft chime, they threw them off.

"You're gonna get cold lying naked on the floor like that," Serge insisted and covered them again.

A louder chime followed and a more insistent blanket toss. *Huh.* Their skin still felt chilled and maybe that was normal? He didn't think so by the way they kept searching after sun-warmed spots like an elderly cat. After a third blanket toss, he gave up, wishing he had a sunlamp to provide more warmth.

Instead, he turned up the cabin's thermostat and monitored the daylight as it moved across the floor, making sure his patient stayed within the rectangle even after they fell asleep again.

The cabin's oil tank should have been at about three-quarters full still, so they would be fine fuel-wise for a bit. He didn't use much these days. Went to bed early. Didn't cook much for himself and the four-room cabin didn't take much to heat. A few degrees more during the daylight hours wouldn't put much of a dent in the fuel supply.

The cabin had been their attempt, his and Josh's, to live off-grid with an independent water supply, septic tank and as many solar panels as they could afford. In the summer, they grew their own vegetables and in the winters, Josh hunted. While Serge's parents had been unrepentant hippies who had been all about self-reliance and separation from the evils of government, instilling a deep-seated suspicion of government motives in their otherwise modern son, for Josh it had just been a grand adventure.

The local news on the university radio station confirmed that the bodies of his guest's companions had been taken to the medical labs at Pitt. University officials publicly expressed sorrow that they hadn't been able to save the aliens, but Serge was sure that in private they were rubbing their hands with glee to have the specimens fall into their laps. Why the government hadn't simply whisked the bodies away, he couldn't guess. Maybe they couldn't take any more in their labs. Maybe it was some special agreement and the university would only do preliminary studies. Who knew?

Around lunchtime, he helped the alien drink some water, an offering that was greedily accepted. Good, they had that much in common, at least. *Needs water. Needs air. Needs light. So far, so good.* The burned feather-scales had all fallen off by then, leaving a large bare spot from shoulder to mid-ribcage, but the skin underneath didn't appear badly damaged.

While the storm had stopped sometime in the early morning, the snow had blocked the road. The ice underneath would make getting the plow hitched up to the truck and trying to maneuver down the hillside life-threatening. Watch and wait. That was the best he could do for now.

He was just about to get some boots on and clear a path down the front steps when his phone buzzed from the side table. Few people called him these days. Spam callers. Occasionally, someone from the university checking on him. He frowned at the unfamiliar number identified only with an acronym he didn't recognize. *USOAA?*

Some prickling instinct made him answer. "Hello?"

"Serge Kosygin?" The voice was male with that sharp edge that screamed *law enforcement.*

He hesitated half a second, wondering if he could get away with denying it. "Yes?"

"Mr. Kosygin, we understand you called in the pod crash last evening."

"I did. Who is this?"

"This is Agent Harlowe from the Office of Alien Affairs. Mr. Kosygin, did you observe the crash site?"

"Look, I have no idea who you are and I'm not comfortable with this phone call."

"How many bodies were at the crash site, sir?"

Serge scowled at the phone, checked to see his visitor was still doing well, and decided not to lie, exactly. "Two."

"Thank you, Mr. Kosygin. We'll be in touch if we have any more questions."

The call disconnected and Serge was left staring at his phone with his heart pounding and his head buzzing with an adrenaline spike. *That was weird. And concerning. Though maybe they really did just need to confirm stuff. Yeah. Right.*

CHAPTER TWO_

THE FIRST SIGHT OF THE ALIEN BEING HAD alarmed Een, though he truly should have been prepared. They had watched transmissions from this planet before running afoul of the gravity well and he had been able to observe the dominant builder species in communication with one another. But the reality of that alien face up close had been shocking, the strange *faiina*, both wiry and sparse, the absurdly thin *lim* that sat so unnaturally still atop its head—it was a shock to his ailing system that set his respirations heaving.

Soft, though, that deep-toned voice, and the hands had been gentle. A lively intelligence resided in those odd multicolored eyes. Even if the being didn't understand why Een needed the light, he had well-developed powers of observation and enough empathy to deduce that he did. Dangerous to assign familiar emotions to aliens without sufficient data, but it was so tempting to think of the being's actions as connected and mindful.

Harmonious.

The little samples of languages from the planet had been out of context, disconnected sounds his translation implant couldn't process. When he was stronger and could think clearly, he would concentrate on communication issues. For now, he could barely lift his head.

He shivered as the solar rays began to fade in the evening, and the being brought the warm wrappings again. This time, Een didn't protest the coverings since the light was gone and the heat from his rescuer's body was welcome. The sleeping platform was an odd shape, though soft. His aching body welcomed it. Een let his eyes drift shut again, grateful that the alien hummed as it moved about the room. Strange, thin, singular notes, but at least his species could conceive of tones. He had encountered some species who had no ability to process notes or rhythm at all.

Alone. I am so alone. Aal was the one who understood strangers. Laiin was the one who was so brave. And only I am left. The least of us. The one who hid in mundane, everyday decisions, who navigated and procured supplies. The one who was always afraid. I am still afraid with no one to tell my fears to, no one to continue the struggle for. Why reach for the light when there is nothing left to illuminate?

Yet he still reached, still struggled to survive. Stubbornness, perhaps, or merely the habit of survival. There would come a time soon when the struggle no longer mattered. He was alone, after all. He could hope for peace in his last days. That would be enough.

———

SERGE SAT IN THE GUESTROOM, strumming his lute, not the fancy Venetian-style one he used for Faires and concerts, but the little six-course one he used for his classes at the university. While he didn't have the academic background for a position as a professor, he'd been hired on as a lecturer ten years before. His specialized skills helped the music department round out its courses, allowing them to offer lute and mandolin and Renaissance dance in the summer sessions. While the department chair had understood his need to take some time off, Serge had to wonder whether they would consider taking him back after his extended absence.

He bent his head over his strings, letting his fingers wander through bits of tunes. Until that moment, he hadn't thought about going back or what came next. Josh would've been furious with his apathy and inaction. *Don't overthink yourself into a funk, Serge. Get up and do something.* He supposed he was. Doing something. A strange, ill-advised something, but maybe in his self-imposed silence, Josh's voice had never left him. Somewhere in the dusty corridors of his mind, Josh had still been whispering all this time.

Do something.

The alien had shown definite signs of settling while Serge was humming, so he took a not-so-wild guess that music might be a point where their cultures intersected. So far, the experiment had gone well, the alien's gaze fixed to Serge's fingers on the strings. Eyes sleepy and half-lidded, the poor alien looked like they were fighting sleep hard, trying to pay attention to the impromptu concert.

He still had no idea whether his guest was male or

female. Probably neither. He, she, or something else entirely had spread out naked on the floor most of the day, making it obvious that there was nothing between those long, slender legs. Not a thing. That didn't mean anything, of course. Genitals didn't have to be external or in the same location. Maybe this species didn't do sexual reproduction at all.

As a geeky kid, he'd wanted to meet aliens but in a Star Trek kind of way—familiar-looking aliens with compatible anatomy who would take him away from the bullies at school and his parents who wanted him to be many things he was not. This situation wasn't at all what he'd envisioned.

Out of habit, he started playing *Greensleeves*. He often used it as the initial demonstration piece, simple and languid, a good showcase for the instrument. It also seemed to get his visitor's attention. The silver eyes opened wider. The hand on the unburned side stroked the side of the bed in time to the music. At first, Serge thought the alien was simply enjoying the music, but as he hit a softer patch, clear notes reached him from across the room, not quite humming, not quite singing, but recreating the refrain pitch-perfect. Serge stopped playing and the alien gave him the lute's notes in response, not merely the melody, but every chord.

The interpretation in an alien voice was eerie and beautiful. Serge held his breath, not wanting to disturb the astounding impromptu concert, awestruck that a single voice could sing three and four notes at once with such bell-clear perfection. The timbre reminded him more of a hang drum than a voice, but the sounds obviously issued from the alien's throat. The notes stopped in mid-refrain and the alien stared at him silently for a moment that stretched Serge's nerves.

When the alien opened their mouth again, the notes they sang had gained vowels and consonants. Serge cocked his head, trying to separate what might have been words. The alien finally waved a hand at their own body, repeating one syllable. *Een.*

"Your name? Een?"

The syllable repeated several times, and Serge realized he was being dense. He couldn't imitate the way Een said it as a C-major chord, but he could sing the bottom note while he plucked the third and the fifth on the lute. Een nestled back into the blankets and Serge interpreted the movement as pleased or at least satisfied.

He pointed to himself. "Serge."

The fronds on Een's head waved and twitched. "Errr," came out as a minor triad.

"Ssssserg-eh." Serge exaggerated the missing letters.

The silver eyes narrowed, perhaps trying to focus on how Serge made the sounds and the next effort was a little better. "Ssserd."

Serge smiled and nodded. "Close enough. I'll take it."

He played a few more songs, humming along when Een picked up the melodies and harmonies. Maybe they didn't have words, but words didn't have a monopoly on communication. Soon Een's eyes closed and their notes quieted to slow respirations, breathing something soft and warm to life in Serge's chest, the warmth occupying a raw, aching spot where he didn't necessarily want it.

The house, not much more than a cabin, had

echoed in its emptiness since Josh had died, a giant gourd from which someone had scooped all of the insides and left the shell to rot in terrible, gray silence.

It had all been too obvious after the fact, the aching joints, the fevers, the sudden loss of what had been a bottomless appetite, but Josh had dredged up one excuse after the other. It was a cold or lingering flu, there was something going around campus, anything to avoid making a doctor's appointment. Between the eventual diagnosis and the end had been a horrible three-month whirlwind, the lymphoma dragging Josh under almost too fast for him to put up a fight. Then one morning, Josh didn't wake up and the doctors told Serge that was it. All he could do was sit by the hospital bed, watching the rise and fall of a too-thin ribcage that couldn't belong to his barrel-bear of a man, holding his hand until the breaths stopped.

No dramatic scenes of medical intervention or wailing and crying, no last flailing struggle to hang onto life, the breaths just stopped. Confusion, anger, guilt and pain paralyzed Serge in that terrible moment, howling through him in jagged shards of rusted iron. He sat there, unable to react as the doctor pronounced time of death, as they asked him questions he couldn't answer. Josh had no living family, no one to interfere in any way, either to wrest Josh away from him or to help Serge through the miasma of his dying.

He'd asked for cremation and was eventually handed a brass urn, no fuss, no funeral full of crying friends, and everything about Josh's death was so fucking *quiet* on the outside while a shrieking hurricane battered Serge's insides. But the world around him had gone still, deafeningly still, so he took a leave of absence from his teaching position and spread Josh's ashes in the woods he had loved, leaving the urn under a mountain laurel like he was setting up some pagan shrine. Maybe he had been.

The anger had died slowly, raging at first, then whimpering, anger over the what-ifs and might-have-beens, but the rest remained like a mold infestation under Serge's skin. With a start, he realized that evening had been the first time he'd picked up his lute since Josh's death. It had taken someone else's need for him to start pulling his head out of his self-pitying ass. Odd that this someone wasn't even human, or maybe that wasn't odd at all. There were days when he felt disconnected from humanity, like a lost button that had fallen out of the big mason jar of just-in-case sewing flotsam and jetsam that sat by the toaster.

Serge got up quietly to put away his lute and go to bed, relatively certain his guest wasn't moving until morning.

———

INPUT. Een needed input. His host—Serd—had left water by the sleeping platform. Feeling strong enough for absorption rather than ingestion, Een shoved a *lim* into the mouth of the container and forced himself to stay still until he'd absorbed all the water. The water here tasted sharp and strange, not at all like the flat, musty recycled station water to which he'd become accustomed. Whatever chemicals or minerals gave it extra heft hadn't made him ill. Another issue resolved.

He crawled from the sleeping platform into the patch of morning light. Morning. He hadn't been on a planet's surface with *mornings* since he'd been small. Waving his *lim* in negation, admonishing himself to stop focusing on minutiae, he examined the room for any signs of communication devices, anything he could use to begin absorbing information.

The room contained little beyond the sleeping platform and the seat Serd had used while he spoke using that lovely instrument. Movement was still excruciating, the bruising beneath his skin, the burns that had begun to weep sticky *rah*, his system fighting hard to repair the damage. One limb at a time worked best, slow movements on his knees. He wasn't ready to try to stand yet. Not far from the rectangle of morning light, recessed shelves ran along the bottom half of the wall, shelves with...what were they? Manuals? Data cards? It was clumsy to take them down one-handed and he dropped the first one, his gaze flicking guiltily toward the doorway. When he picked the little rectangle up again, it was undamaged, but its leaves didn't help him decipher use or meaning.

Carefully, he took rectangles down and replaced them one by one, until he opened a larger one that contained not only the strange, stiff alien characters, but also beautiful images. This one was potentially more helpful. The images of life forms had to be from this planet. As far as Een knew, the dominant builder species had only the most rudimentary off-planet technology, so a catalog of life forms from other planets would be unlikely. If this book was a catalog of native species, perhaps with the classifications listed underneath, his language implant might have a starting point. Een moved back to his spot of light and sat carefully, balancing his find on his knees, and began to leaf through, completely absorbed by the beauty and variety of life displayed for him.

A shift in air currents and scent alerted him to his host in the doorway. Serd stood motionless, still as a piece of Antonian digital art, and Een had a bad moment wondering if perhaps he had perpetrated some terrible breach of etiquette by looking at the image manual. Then Serd continued into the room, and the anxious knot in Een's core gave a bit. Serd spoke in that flat, tuneless way, though it was a deep, warm sound like an air circulator humming. While Een couldn't understand meaning or intention, the voice comforted him.

"My breath greets yours," Een said in answer to whatever Serd said. He could still be polite, even if they had no language in common yet.

Frustrating, the lack of a language interface, the lack of any tools to help him decipher this new world. He held up the image collection to Serd, hoping that this might be a start. Serd cocked his head and set aside the pile of textiles he carried before he joined Een at the window. He held a round vessel out to Een, gesturing for him to take it. Since he had no idea what to do with it, Een pushed it gently back toward his host.

Serd solved the mystery by picking up the metal utensil stuck in whatever steaming mess was in the vessel and popping it in his mouth. *Ah. Ingestion.* That answered one question, at least. Serd's species were matter-consumers. While the ingestion of other life forms was repulsive to Een on a purely physical level, he had nothing against matter-consumers. Some of his closest acquaintances on the station had needed biomatter to survive. He was simply disappointed that the dominant species on this planet was not photophagic like himself.

He lifted the manual toward Serd again. "What are these? Can you read the names?"

No, Serd wouldn't understand the words, but perhaps he would comprehend that there was a question. The strange shaggy head bent over the open pages, and Serd pointed to the image of a yellow and white life form, saying something in his flat, single tone voice.

Een pointed to the symbols underneath the image, running his finger over them. "Can you read it for me? Tell me the words?"

He repeated the action several times and Serd's eyes widened. He began to point to the words, speaking slowly and softly. Een clutched the bare finger and moved it over the words again, silently asking him to repeat the sounds.

"Shaza daezee," Een finally tried the words, pleased when Serd bobbed his head up and down.

At least, he'd puzzled that out as an affirmative gesture. He ran Serd's finger over the symbols underneath, words that most likely contained information about the shaza daezee, and Serd read those as well, his patience seemingly unending. Serd's warmth was welcome nestled close to him and Een dared to feel a spark of companionship, despite the dangers of such assumptions. Serd might be planning to eat him or vivisect him the next day. Een might suddenly stumble over something that gave unforgivable offense, and find himself abandoned in the wild. Until he understood more, he couldn't afford the luxury of assigning motives to actions.

The language implant began to process, slowly building symbols in relation to sound. Meaning would come over time, with context, but the beginning filled Een with hope that he might not be entirely mute and helpless for long.

———

EEN HAD REFUSED both the oatmeal and the pajamas, both of which would have worried Serge if they weren't obviously improving hour by hour. It didn't make sense to Serge that they were more alert and moving better without any fuel besides the little bit of water they drank, but they were. When the sun moved from the guestroom, Serge carried them to the front room again, the guide to North American wildflowers clutched to Een's chest.

His heart had nearly stopped when he'd spotted the book in alien hands, Josh's last work, with his painstaking photographs and descriptions. Serge had accepted the book, published posthumously, from the university. He'd set it reverently on the shelf with Josh's other books and hadn't been able to bring himself to touch it since. But Een didn't know that. How could they? Serge had gathered his misplaced anger, shoved it somewhere dark, and sat beside Een to read the words written by a beloved hand. Forever lost and stilled, but in this, preserved. Josh had poured so much of himself into that book, each photograph a spot of time, each paragraph a morsel of that sharp, fiercely independent mind.

Serge's fingers had trembled at first, his voice shaking as he tried to read words that kept blurring on the page. It was Een, warm from the sun, insistent in their need, who helped him continue. Before long, Serge had been smiling, knowing that Josh would've loved his book used as a primer and as an instrument of first contact with Earth's biodiversity.

Sitting with Een, a naked being covered in feather-scales with tubular snakes on his head, had *calmed* Serge. Not something he wanted to look at too closely right then, though Een's melodic humming probably had something to do with it.

Een still hummed in his box of light on the floor, leafing carefully through Josh's book, while Serge stared out the window. The snow was melting already. He probably could make it into the city safely later that afternoon.

I should take Een to the university. They really should be the professors' problem, not mine.

The thought brought a flush of shame faster than a copperhead strike. Een wasn't a problem. They were a person, one who was struggling to communicate and probably wouldn't do well in an environment full of authority figures and bureaucratic types *insisting* that they communicate. No, it made more sense to let them stay in the cabin's quiet environs until they were more mobile and had their bearings. It was only right, and it wasn't as if Serge was hiding them from the authorities.

Though if he thought too hard about it, he really was.

The thought of handing Een over felt wrong, as if they were a stray puppy who had needed help and Serge was considering taking them to the closest shelter. Not that he thought of Een as a homeless canine. Een was his guest and it sure as hell was wrong to take a *guest* to a kill shelter.

Since early spring, the government had held televised press conferences, stating clearly that the landing aliens were to be met with compassion and every possible assistance. Serge didn't trust it. Not entirely. Not everything his parents taught him growing up had stuck, but he couldn't help the constant hum of mistrust for government entities itching beneath his skin. Maybe they would treat Een well and allow them to live their own life. More likely they'd be a lab rat, poked and prodded, kept in a sterile room.

I can't betray them like that. Until they can figure out what's going on around them, I'll protect them.

CHAPTER THREE_

THE FROZEN PRECIPITATION MELTED QUICKLY, so
the pod's information on weather truly had been
within normal margins. The season was, in general,
warming. Serd had pulled a comfortable seating
platform in front of the large window and Een spent
much of the daylight hours there, fascinated by the
birth of new life outside the dwelling.

All sorts of *nila* broke through the ground, green
fingerlings reaching for the sun, the sheer exuberance
of sudden life making Een wish he had his instruments
to measure the soil composition, the growth rates, the
electrical activity... The pain under his skin flared, loss
and isolation. He would never have anyone to annoy
with his excited trills about new species again. A short
triad of pain escaped that he choked off self-
consciously, glancing behind him. His chords and
scales of pain seemed to upset Serd. Better to try to
keep them quiet.

Lacking his instruments and the strength to go
outside, Een could only speculate regarding the

sentience of the life he assumed was photophagic outside the window. No observable parenting behaviors manifested in any of the larger, established life forms, so sentience might have been limited to defense and reproduction. Perhaps the huge, looming beings set back from the dwelling were more complex, thinking beings, merely dormant in the cold. Would their young sprout after they emerged from hibernation? What sort of communication system did that imply? Possibly the larger beings didn't begin reproduction at all until the cold season ended.

Serd slid onto the seating platform beside him to offer a container of water and join Een in his observation. The soft alien hand slid against his to hand over the water and Een closed his fingers around Serd's naked ones in a gesture of gratitude. How Serd interpreted it was unclear, but he wasn't obviously disturbed, sitting quietly beside Een and stroking the back of his hand gently. They sat together in near silence until Serd got up for his midday nourishment, and when he returned, he had brought another species manual, this one specific to the larger, many-branched beings.

After some fumbling about with the pages, Serd read a word underneath one of the beings, then pointed out the window at the one closest to the dwelling. He repeated it several times, obviously waiting for Een to try it.

The word was a single beat with familiar consonants. "Ferr."

Serd's lips tipped up on one side, a facial expression Een couldn't parse yet, and repeated the word. Een fixated on his mouth, the way his throat moved, the quality of sound.

He adjusted and tried again. "Furr."

This time Serd bobbed his head up and down, a gesture Een recognized by now as approval as well as affirmation. Another few pages on, Serd pointed to a being of a different shape and appendages. The word for this one was another single beat but ended in one of those strange sounds Een couldn't puzzle out.

"Ooa."

Serd shook his head back and forth and repeated the sound. Frustrated, Een stabbed repeatedly at the image with his finger, hoping Serd would understand that he should keep repeating, while Een put a hand on either side of Serd's face. Tri-color eyes widened, the black centers enlarging. Surprise? Fear? But Serd didn't pull away. He moved Een's hands gently, sliding them to where his jaw met his throat.

The strange sound, a sort of click, originated in Serge's throat. No. At the back of his mouth.

Een placed the back of his tongue against the roof of his mouth, trying to imitate the sound. "Ooad."

Again, Serd repeated the syllable, opening his mouth farther for Een to observe. Farther back, that last sound. A sudden shiver raced through Een's *faiina*. This close, Serd's heat was astounding, almost better than the sunlight. His scent was a strange mix of his cleansing solutions and what must have been the natural scent of his species, warm and complex, not at all unpleasant. Een's *lim* reached forward before he was conscious of them moving, the tendrils yearning toward Serd, attracted both to his soft vibrations and to the enticing particulates of his scent. *No. You react because you are alone and desolate. Your biological makeups aren't in any way compatible. Stop this.*

His notes still trembled as he tried again. "Ooag."

Serd inclined his head once. Apparently, that had been closer to the correct sound. Troubled by his body's reactions, mortified by how he struggled with the language, Een pointed to the page, his implant parsing some of the symbols into sounds for him. "Wide Ooag."

Eyes wide, Serd leaned in to look at the page and repeated both words before he leaned back to stare at Een. His sudden departure from the window startled Een so badly that his *lim* nearly twisted into knots atop his head. Offended? Angry? Upset? What had he done?

When Serd came back, though, he appeared calm and clutched a gray rectangle in both hands. He reclaimed his spot beside Een and demonstrated that the rectangle split, one half opening perpendicular to the other. Lighted images appeared on the vertical screen.

"Data?" In his excitement, Een had forgotten again that Serge wouldn't understand. "Is it a data interface?"

Serd tapped on the device's symbol board until the screen showed a row of images, more of the planet's life forms. He showed Een how to open the entry for each image and then, most wonderful of all, showed him how to prompt the device to verbalize the writing, lighting up each word as it spoke. Overjoyed, Een stroked Serd's face with his *lim*, forgetting once again that he dealt with an alien culture. Serd jerked back out of reach, so it was a mistake, but either Serd was an extraordinarily accepting member of his species or the error was a small one. He patted Een's shoulder and left him with the tech device.

The data storage was everything Een needed since it contained both language in text and extended examples in conversation, stories, presumably, and other interactions. He found it fascinating that they spoke with rhythm and melody when they held various tone instruments, but without those, they spoke in the tuneless way Serd normally used. As his implant processed, comprehension increased bit by bit. Structurally, the languages were accessible, with some irregularities but for the most part governed by clear rules. His struggles were all in the imitation of language, many sounds made by alien mouths and throats that he found impossible to replicate.

When Serd wandered back in from whatever chore had occupied his time outside the dwelling, Een tried a bit of the alien language.

"I am Een. I am Aalana."

Serd stopped blowing on his poor naked hands and stared. Then the corners of his mouth turned up. *Smile.* The expression was called a smile. "I am Serge. I am huemon."

Huemon... Een tapped on the symbol board and the data device corrected him. Human. He brought up images of more natives like Serd...Serjeh and pointed to the screen. "Humans?"

"Yes." Serjeh still smiled, nodding. "All of them."

Confirmation of successful communication—they had exchanged species names. Serjeh sat down with him again and exchanged other words. The thin strands on his head were hair, as was the strange, patchy *faiina* on various parts of his body. Humans had no *lim*, and their hair had none of the *lims'* sensitivities. Neither, Een discovered when Serjeh accessed information on human anatomy, was the hair in any way involved in reproduction.

Two-gendered reproduction wasn't a new concept for him, of course. Neither was internal embryo development. Serge conveyed through images that he was a pollinator. Een managed to explain that he was also a pollinator, though his language skills weren't complex enough to explain Aalana genders and reproduction especially since human anatomy was so puzzling. The placement of the human pollinator gender's reproductive organs seemed problematic and though Serjeh wore coverings, the organs still seemed dangerously exposed.

However, all evolutions had some logical impetus. Een simply didn't understand the environmental pressures and ecological history of the planet well enough yet. He was pleased that he had the means to learn now. Serjeh had understood and had provided the tools, and Een began to feel that it was quite unlikely he would be eaten.

CHAPTER FOUR_

TWO THINGS BOTHERED SERGE AS HE WATCHED the evening news with Een. No, three. Not Een, of course, snuggled up against him on the couch, happy to cocoon under a fleece blanket now the sun had set. Serge had admitted to himself that he *liked* having Een cuddle with him. His company was soothing instead of irritating, which Serge hadn't experienced with anyone recently. He liked Een as a person, which wasn't the easiest thing for him to admit to himself.

No, the niggles in his brain all pointed in the same general direction. That call from the government agency weighed on his mind. That can't have been the end of it. When they came for Een, he would try to hide him and do his best to lie, because they would come.

The second thing bothering him was the agency itself, the Office of Alien Affairs. Their director was onscreen now, giving a news conference to update the press on the aliens. He reassured the press, again, that the aliens were peaceful and all seemed to be refugees.

Yes, communication was still difficult. Yes, the aliens were safe and well cared for.

"Een? The people he's showing pictures of, other people who landed—do you know them?"

After an interrogatory chime, Een asked, "Know? Friends?"

"Well, yeah, that too." Serge took Een's reaching hand, his thumb automatically stroking the soft *faiina* on his palm. *Soothing. God, yes.* "But if they weren't you're friends, do you recognize them? Have you seen them before?"

"Seen. Yes. People." Een pointed to the ones who looked like manta rays. "Mnep." Then to the ones who looked like stick bundles. "Dalidana."

Serge took that to mean that those were the names of the aliens as groups rather than individual names. "Okay. So you know what they look like. Do they look okay to you? Healthy? Not scared? Afraid?"

"Mnep color is...not correct." Een snuggled closer and Serge put an arm around him. "Not afraid."

All right. They were still photos, so it was probably hard for Een to tell much, though he didn't seem distressed by any of the pictures. Serge would've felt a lot better if one of the aliens had stepped up to the podium to say, *We're fine. Everyone's been really nice and helpful.*

Until that happened, until the aliens themselves got on TV and said they were fine, like they had in Iceland, Serge couldn't let himself believe it. Pain speared his chest at the thought of Een vanishing into the OAA system, never to be see again. He hugged Een close, gently moving a *lim* over that had wandered in front of his eyes. *I won't let them take you. Promise.*

. . .

THE NEXT MORNING while Een worked away diligently at gathering more vocabulary, Serge decided to tackle his second niggle. The Aalana bodies from Een's pod—why Pitt? Why hadn't they gone to the feds? Though he needed to be careful whom he talked to and what he said. Serge's own contacts in the music department were useless for this, but Josh's friends from the school of medicine were a better bet.

Josh had been biology, of course, so normally there wouldn't have been much overlap. But Josh tended to get involved and had served in the University Senate. He knew *everyone* and had even guest lectured about medicinal plants in some of the pharmacology classes. Parties, dinners, nights out— Serge did know a handful of the medical faculty personally. He could even call a couple of them friends, though he'd only been a friend by association.

It's just a phone call. Nothing to be nervous about. Still his heart hammered as he stepped out onto the porch and called the department. His knees buckled in relief when a familiar admin answered.

"Donna? Hi, it's Serge Kosygin."

"Mr. Kosygin? How *are* you? Is everything all right?"

There it was. The reason he'd stopped calling anyone. The heavy sympathy in her voice, the pity, it had grated on his last frayed nerve. *We were all so sorry to hear. If there's anything we can do. Such a terrible loss.* They meant well, he reminded himself and took a deep breath.

"I'm doing fine, Donna. Thanks. Um, is Dr. Ahmal around? Or maybe Dr. Carver?"

"Let me check the schedule... Dr. Ahmal has office hours now. Did you want me to put you through?"

"Please. I appreciate it."

The next voice on the line was a pleasant, cultured baritone, "This is Dr. Ahmal."

"Omar? It's, um, Serge."

A hint of a smile crept into that familiar voice. "You don't sound like you're sure. It's been weeks, Serge. How are you managing?"

"I'm...I'm okay." It sounded surprisingly like the truth. "I have a question. Probably kind of a weird question."

"Of course." Omar huffed a laugh. "I didn't think you were calling just to say hello."

Heat flooded Serge's face. He was a terrible friend and he knew it. That didn't make the phone call any easier. "I'm sorry, Omar. I mean to call..."

"No, sorry. That was out of line." Omar drew in a sharp breath. "You've been deeply depressed this past year. It wasn't up to *you* to stay in touch and I *am* glad to hear from you. So what's your strange question?"

"You know I found the—" Serge almost slipped and said the Aalana pod. "The alien pod that crashed near here, right?"

"Right. Of course."

"And the news said there were two bodies. They went to the university?"

"They did. Serge, where is this going?"

Serge hesitated. Omar was a friend. He really was. He was the one person who'd bothered to come up to the cabin to check on Serge after Josh died. But still,

Serge felt a need for caution. Friends sometimes did things *for your own good*. "I've been watching the news. And seeing this new federal agency that's for the aliens. Why didn't the bodies go to them?"

"Well. That's actually a good question, not a weird one." Something tapped on the other end, probably a pen against Omar's desk. "One of the issues was the possible fragility of the bodies. The agency wanted to get them to the nearest appropriately equipped facility as quickly as possible. They weren't willing to risk cross-country transport. The other part of it... Serge, you have to promise that this stays between us."

Serge's conspiracy feelers shot up to attention. "Whatever it is. Yeah. Promise."

"It's a little embarrassing, but it's simple nepotism. Our provost is the brother-in-law of the OAA's director. He made noises about the university being a better place for transparency and for PR, but it's plain that the agency caved to his demands because of family relations."

"Oh." That wasn't at all what Serge had been expecting. "Oh. Well. I guess it's a real coup for your department, right?"

Omar laughed out loud this time. "Yes, but now we're dealing with all the territorial contests. Who gets to do the research? How many people will have access? Does Bio get to have a hand in? Chemistry? Anthro? Let the games begin."

"Hooray for academic pissing contests."

"You said it. My money's on Kurt Phillip's getting the project. He does have the most interdisciplinary proposal."

"And he's bullheaded enough to get what he

wants," Serge grumbled. Kurt was a bit of a cold fish, at least what Serge had seen.

"Let's say persistent, at least. Serge, I have students coming in. I'll call you soon, all right?"

"Okay." Normally he would've left it at that, but with Een staying with him, he'd started to feel more, well, *human* again. He realized that he actually missed talking to Omar. "Sounds good. Thanks, Omar."

They said their goodbyes and Serge stayed out on the porch for a few minutes even though the breeze was starting to cut through his shirt. The government, for whatever reason, pick one, had let the Aalana go to civilians. That had to mean something. Maybe it just meant the bodies were too damaged to be useful? He shuddered, worried for the other aliens in government custody all over again.

———

"Serjeh?" Een placed a hand on Serjeh's shoulder, the shivering all too evident under his touch. "Cold?"

"Yes. And you can't say it yet even if I hear you thinking it, but yes, I'm being an idiot and standing out here without a jacket." Serjeh turned them and went back inside with Een.

While Een had been concerned about Serjeh's unprotected skin out in the cold, his wildly waving *lim* betrayed his excitement. He kept hold of Serjeh's hand and pulled him to the laptop on the window seat where a vid was playing. Serjeh lifted the laptop to get a better view and Een stabbed a finger at the screen where humans moved to music. For a full minute and a half, Een sang in his own language about the lovely movement song before he started searching for human words.

"Humans..." Een flailed a moment. "Move harmony!"

"Singing with movement?" Serjeh nodded. "That's a good way of looking at it. We call it dance." He pointed to the screen and repeated the word. "Dance."

"Danz?"

"Dance."

Een trilled his joy, his *lim* tingling as they brushed Serjeh's head. "Dans. Serjeh teach? Human dans?"

"I can't do that," Serjeh laughed as he pointed to the humans making graceful leaps. "But I can teach you something else."

Carefully, Serjeh moved Een's *lim* aside, the touch sending a warm rush through him and all his *lim* yearned toward Serjeh as he moved away. Een concentrated, bringing the wayward appendages under control. He wasn't an adolescent, unable to separate a comforting touch from desire, even if he still leaned toward where Serjeh had walked to the other side of the room. He watched Serjeh's movements in fascination as he pulled a shining disk from a square box and fed it into one of the devices on the flat surface beside the viewing screen.

Music filled the room, slow and peaceful. A version of Serjeh's lude played, but others too, some of them with the sound of breath instruments and rhythmic instruments. Serjeh returned and placed Een's hand atop his.

"This is what I teach...taught..." Een couldn't parse the momentary twist of Serjeh's lips. It wasn't a smile. It seemed the opposite of one. Then he said an incomprehensible word followed by *music and dance.*

"Teach? Young humans?"

Serjeh tipped his free hand back and forth. "Not small, but not quite adult. I'll teach you a slow one I start with. No jumping for you yet. Not with those burns. Follow my steps. Do as I do."

A step forward with the right foot, then the left—step, together, step, together. Serjeh stepped sideways, Een tried to follow and was motioned the other way. Next the same steps backward, then Serjeh pressed their palms together and they circled each other with slow steps. The opposite palms pressed together to circle the other way.

All the while, Serjeh held Een's gaze. Those eyes, so alien, so strange and beautiful. He had marveled at them before, wondered over the function of each separate color, but now... They held a warmth that was more than kindness, a weight that was more than concern. Een fought his *lim's* reactions, more and more common in Serjeh's presence. Attraction? Certainly something that happened between different galactic peoples, but Een hadn't thought it possible for him.

When Serjeh ended the movement song, Een wrapped his arms around his host's neck in a thank you, surprised when Serjeh reciprocated with gentle warmth. Een let his breath out on a soft chord, melting against Serjeh, simply concentrating on their mingled breath, letting all his spinning thoughts go.

———

THE NEXT MORNING started in the newly usual way—

Een in the front room with water, sun and laptop, and Serge in the kitchen making himself breakfast. Serge caught himself smiling at the thought that any of this could be called *usual*, but as strange as it all was, it felt comfortable and right.

He was just bringing his plate of eggs and scrapple scramble out to sit with Een when the sound of an engine climbing the hill caught his attention. A half-jog to the front window got him there in time to spot a black SUV headed toward the cabin, tinted windows and something about its frame screaming federal agents.

"Een, let's move you back to your room for a bit," Serge put an arm around Een, made sure he had his laptop and water, and steered him back to the guest room. "There are humans coming. I'm not sure if they're, um, good humans or not."

All Een's *lim* increased their waving. "Serjeh? Danger?"

"I don't *think* so. But please stay here." Serge helped him sit in the rectangle of light on the floor, motioning with his hands to back up his words. "Stay quiet. No sounds. No notes, please."

While this obviously distressed Een with his *faiina* starting to spike, he gave Serge a nod.

"Thank you. It'll be okay, Een." Serge closed the door, hoping he hadn't just lied.

He wanted so bad to go back and comfort Een until those spikes settled into feather-scales again, but he was out of time. The sharp raps of a law enforcement knock were already sounding on the front door.

Serge took a deep breath, put on his best puzzled expression, and opened the door. "Can I help you?"

There were four of them, agents in agent suits and mirror shades, the outlines of shoulder holsters not at all subtle under their jackets. They'd retreated down the steps, maybe to give him some space. The one in front held up a badge. "Mr. Kosygin? Serge Kosygin?"

"Yes. That's me." No reason to deny that, at least.

Front agent came up onto the porch and waved a hand at her colleagues. "I'm Special Agent Saunders. These are Agents Feldhauer, Marshall and Curtis. I'll get right to the point, sir. On the night of April twenty-first, you called in a crash landing of an alien vessel, is that true?"

"I did, ma'am, yes."

"But you failed to remain at the site to wait for the authorities."

Serge suppressed a flinch at the word *failed*. Already, she implied he'd done something wrong. "I couldn't do anything to help the crash victims. It was snowing heavily. Roads were treacherous." He nodded to his pickup. "My truck's not a Sno-Cat or something. They would've been rescuing me next if I'd stayed out there."

"I see. But you had driven out to the crash site in treacherous weather."

"I was on my way home and saw the ship come down. Are you going somewhere with this, Agent... Sanders, was it?" He had no idea why he was trying to annoy her. It was probably a bad idea.

"Saunders," she corrected sharply. "Mr. Kosygin, there were two bodies recovered at the crash site."

"Yes. I saw them. Poor things."

"Did you take a look at the bodies?"

Serge shrugged. "Just enough to see there wasn't anything I could do."

"I'm going to be blunt, Mr. Kosygin." Agent Saunders took off her mirror shades to reveal sharp gray eyes that were the antithesis of warm and fuzzy. "Did you take anything from the crash site?"

He didn't have to fake his shock. "Of course not. That would've been robbing a corpse."

Saunders tapped her shades against her palm. "Why don't you tell me exactly what you saw, sir."

"Sure. I saw the pod coming down, too fast for a safe landing. It was on fire when it crashed. By the time I got to the site, a lot had already burned. The... canopy, I guess, was open. Two aliens were lying in the snow at bad angles, so I thought they might've been thrown out when they crashed. One was charred. That was bad. The other was lying all twisted. They were aliens, but you could tell they weren't supposed to bend that way."

"You checked? Made certain they were dead?"

Serge blew out a shaky breath. It was hard remembering that night—he didn't have to lie about that either. "Look, I'm not a doctor. They weren't moving. They weren't breathing. The authorities were on their way to make sure, but to me it looked like they didn't make it."

More palm tapping and a long, hard stare later, Agent Saunders backed up a step so she wasn't crowding Serge. She reached into her pocket and handed him a card. "Thank you, Mr. Kosygin. That's all for today. You remember anything else you think we should know, call me."

"All right. I will." Serge waved the card at the silent backup agents. "You folks be careful going down the mountain. Probably some ice still."

He watched them drive away, the sick feeling never leaving his stomach. What had they really wanted? What was it they knew?

CHAPTER FIVE_

A week after Een's rescue, the weather decided to concede that it might be spring. Serge was outside checking the level in the oil tank when Een wandered onto the front porch, stark naked and barefoot. Naked was probably overstating the case since Een's beautiful lilac dragon scale *faiina* were just as good as feathers or fur.

"Een?" Serge called over to get his attention and pointed to his own boots. "Shoes?"

Silver eyes, like twin pools of mercury, blinked at him. Een stared at the indicated footwear, then stared at his feet. "Not..." He waved vaguely up at the sky and sang in his multitoned voice, his t's still softened nearly to d's. "Out atmosphere. Not...needing?"

"It's not freezing out here, but it's not warm yet."

Een tipped one corner of his mouth up, his hesitant imitation of a smile, and shook his head. Scary, in a way, the speed at which Een acquired language and human gestures. Maybe it was some special adaptation. Traveling through space, he might have run into other species regularly.

"You don't feel cold?"

"Sun." Een spread his arms and moved onto the porch steps, into the full sunlight. "More."

"You greedy thing." Serge chuckled as he replaced the cap on the oil tank. "Taking all the sunlight."

"It is not..." Een hesitated, head tipped to one side. "Humor?"

"Yes." Serge settled on the top step, patting the wood for Een to sit with him. Some forms of humor, like sarcasm, seemed too alien for Een to grasp, but others he picked up, so humor itself wasn't a foreign concept.

"Eating your star," Een said with the little trill that Serge believed was something like a laugh. He eased down beside Serge with little hissing chirps.

While the *faiina* were already growing back over the burns, some movements obviously still caused him pain. The scales were soft today, more like feathers as the breeze ruffled them. When Een startled, they grew hard and spiky, providing natural armor, but as he calmed again, the blood flow, or whatever caused the defensive change, decreased and they lay flat again, soft as chick fluff.

He nestled against Serge as he so often did, probably taking comfort in shared warmth even if he claimed he wasn't cold. Serge took his hand, the now-familiar six long fingers with their smooth, catlike pads, because Een took comfort in this as well. Not that he was completely selfless. Een's hand felt good in his, like it belonged there. He had wondered if all Aalana were so physically demonstrative, but it didn't matter. This was what Een needed and Serge found himself more and more compelled, willingly so, to give Een everything his happiness required.

"That person is...distressed," Een said, gazing toward the left side of the house.

Distressed was a new word, so Serge wasn't certain how Een meant it, and there was no person in sight. He pointed to the tree near the corner of the house. "The holly?"

"Yes. Holly. She has no..." Een struggled, twittering in an unhappy way. "To...what word? To make more like her?"

"She? But that tree never had berries." Serge stopped himself before he could say anything else stupid. Of course. There weren't any other hollies nearby. A female needed a male holly to make berries. "Reproduce, Een. She needs a male to reproduce. I guess I need to get her a boyfriend."

Een tried the new word slowly, carefully imitating the consonants. "Two...to re-produce? Always?"

"For hollies? There could be more. But male and female, yes." They had talked about male and female concerning humans, so this shouldn't have been a new concept either.

"Always two? For..." Een waved a hand at the woods around them. "All persons?"

Serge opened his mouth, and closed it when he realized he had to think about that. "Many..." He waved his hand at the surrounding trees as well. "Many people need two. Male and female to mate. Not always." Snowdrops bloomed beside the steps and he pointed those out to Een. "Sometimes male and female are on one species...person. Some people, ones too small to see, don't need male and female and reproduce by splitting."

Een hummed softly, taking the information in. He would most likely be back on the laptop when they went back inside, looking up more on reproduction. "Serjeh? Mate? You?"

An icy fist clutched tight around Serge's heart at the question. He managed a breath, then another, and found that, yes, he could breathe past the molasses-thick knot of sorrow in his throat. "I had a mate. Sometimes humans don't mate to reproduce. They mate because they love each other."

"Love?"

"Hard to explain." Serge let out another long breath, trying to think of concepts Een might understand. "Because you fit together. Because the other person fills in...holes in your music."

"Harmony."

"Yes. Perfect, beautiful harmony. My mate was male, like me. He died."

Een nodded slowly. "I had mates also. Also died."

"Mates? How many?"

"Two," Een sang softly, his notes dissolving into that heart-tugging dirge he had sung the night Serge brought him home.

In that moment, with the wind singing counterpoint to Een's minor chords, Serge understood. The two other Aalana killed so horribly in the crash, those had been Een's mates.

"Oh, Een. I'm so sorry," Serge whispered and pulled him close. They clung together, each weeping in his own way for the loves they had lost, rocking and clutching each other tight, two bereft souls washed up together on the swells of the galaxy's storms.

So different, so foreign to each other, and yet in this, each understood the other's bone-deep pain without words. Een stroked Serge's hair, his dirge quieting to single plaintive notes while Serge's breath hitched on the last updrafts of sobs.

"You are alone," Een finally sang softly.

Serge pulled back to look at him as Een's *lim* gently caressed his face, the strange serpentine organs brushing his skin in cobweb-soft touches that set fireflies in Serge's stomach. "I have been. I was. But with you here, we're alone together. And I guess that's not as bad as being alone by myself."

He couldn't imagine that had made much sense to Een since it hardly made sense to Serge, but Een nestled next to him again with his head on Serge's shoulder.

"Better," Een said in a multitoned murmur, so he'd certainly made his own sense out of Serge's babbling.

High above them, a jet's roar, muted by distance, rumbled above them as it left a vapor trail across thin, rippled clouds. Serge wondered who was on that plane and where they were going. Were they going toward loved ones or away? Was it a happy occasion that made them climb into a silver canister that hurtled them across the sky? Was it business or was it something tragic and terrible? He shook his head and came back down to earth, to his front porch and Een beside him.

Een was right. It was better together.

————

OVER THE NEXT TWO DAYS, Een buried himself in computer articles on mating and different kinds of reproduction, on friendship and love, sometimes with Serge's help on the searches, though more often struggling on his own. He had such a fierce need for knowledge that it humbled Serge. His own studies had never been so feverish or so all-consuming.

Een learned enough to convey what Serge had suspected—that Een's body refueled on a type of photosynthesis. While he couldn't bring himself to think of Een as a plant, his physiology resembled plant over animal in at least his digestive and circulatory systems. Serge had seen for himself that Een didn't bleed. He oozed like a damaged tree.

Not that differences in bodily functions bothered Serge. Een's kindness, his patience and his ability to accept those not like him were far more important. During the day, Een read or listened to the computer read to him. In the evenings, they danced together and Serge taught him songs that Een learned after a single hearing and gave back to Serge augmented with additional harmonies. They played together, Serge on his lute and Een on his own vocal chords, until Een dropped off to sleep.

A word described the strange lulling routine into which Serge's life had fallen, though it took him some time to think of it. Peace. The pain wasn't gone, but the terrible buzzing disorientation of raw grief had quieted to a low-level hum. Life was peaceful and warmed somehow. Brighter.

Maybe too much so, since Serge managed to forget about the world outside his property lines until the black SUV rumbled up the hill toward the house.

They were back and he hadn't heard them approaching. Fucking agents. Why couldn't they leave him and Een alone?

"Een. Een!" Serge called out as he hurried back inside. "Go to your room, please. Close the door. Stay there until I come for you. Please."

Een placed the laptop on the bench seat by the front window, rising slowly as his *lim* began to dance crazy patterns around his head. "Serjeh? You are frightened again?"

"Yes. It's the people who came before. They might mean you harm. I don't want you to go with them. Do you understand? I don't want them to know you're here. Please hide."

With a last glance out the window at the oncoming vehicle, Een shut the laptop, perhaps thinking an open laptop would be suspicious when Serge had been outside, scurried to his room, and shut the door quietly.

Please let this be nothing. Just more questions about the crash. Please stay out of sight, Een.

The government car stopped outside the cabin, its shining black menacing beside Serge's dusty blue truck. All four doors opened, and the expected agents in black suits and mirror shades stepped out. He opened the door before they could pound on it this time, leaning against the doorframe with his arms crossed over his chest. Calm. Confident. Trying to exude *this is my house and you're on my property.*

"You're back. What can I do for you, Agent Sanders?"

"Saunders," she snarled and removed her sunglasses to uncover those raptor-sharp eyes. The other agents had crowded close, blocking the stairs.

"Forensics suggest, sir, that there was a third occupant in that alien pod. You wouldn't happen to know anything about that, would you?"

Damn it. They knew. They were looking for Een specifically. Serge tried for a casual drawl, hoping his voice didn't shake. "No, ma'am. I only saw two."

"Evidence all points to a third occupant. Given the conditions of the first two, the third would most likely have been deceased as well."

"Sounds likely." Serge forced himself not to fidget. *I can do this. I'm a statue. Made of stone.*

Special Agent Saunders took a step forward, the angle of her jaw suddenly aggressive. "Mr. Kosygin, we have tire tracks onsite that match your truck's brand of tire. Lots of boot prints that night, but one set, that I'm willing to bet match the ones by your front door, go directly to where that third body was and have a deeper imprint leaving the site. Now are you *sure* there's nothing you want to tell me?"

"Nope." Serge felt his face heating and knew the red would show in his cheeks. He couldn't help that. "Not a thing."

"Don't know why the hell you'd want to stash a dead alien, but you can't have any *good* reasons. We're searching the premises. Curtis, check his truck. Move aside, sir."

Serge set himself across the doorway, feet spread wide. "I don't see a warrant. You have no right to barge into my house."

One of the other agents, more wall than man, said in a deceptively soft voice, "We're from the Office of Alien Affairs, Mr. Kosygin. We don't need a warrant."

"No! You can't do this!" Serge protested even as the

two largest agents took him by the arms and forcibly moved him out of the doorway. Agent Curtis returned from a quick search of the pickup and assisted. "This is my home! I didn't—" He broke off as Agent Saunders strode for the hallway to the bedrooms. "Een! Get out the window! Run!"

Either Een misunderstood or he completely misread the situation, since a moment later the door to the guest room opened and Een emerged with all his *faiina* bristling.

"Serjeh?"

"Holy shit, he's keeping a live alien prisoner!"

"Damn it, no!" Serge hurled himself between Een and the wall of advancing agents. "He's still recovering. Leave him alone!"

"Stand aside, Mr. Kosygin!" Agent Saunders pulled her service weapon and aimed it in a two-handed, aggressive stance at Serge. "I'm charging you with illegal detainment of an offworld immigrant!"

Behind him, Een placed a hand on his shoulder and sang something in his own language that sounded alarmed. He shoved Serge behind him, the hard, spiking *faiina* on Een's hand scratching Serge's shoulder. Een's *lim*, suddenly engorged and dark violet, all flicked toward the agents. The terrible hissing issuing from Een's throat startled Serge so badly that he stumbled back toward the guest room while the agents hesitated, uncertain in the face of Een's obvious hostility.

The *lim* twitched and quivered. White strings shot from their open ends, spattering the agents clustered at the end of the hallway and a hysterical laugh caught in Serge's throat since it looked as if Een had shot them with Silly String. But the kid stuff in the can didn't have any toxic effects. As soon as the stuff touched skin, the agents jerked in badly managed marionette dances and one by one, hit the floor, convulsing for a few heartbeats before they all lay terribly still.

"Shit...Een. Did you kill them?" Serge whispered.

Een leaned against the wall, his lavender coloration dulled to gray, and shook his head. "I do not know."

"Get to the truck. Hurry. Get inside the cab." Serge's brain whirled through terrible possibilities, but the one screaming the loudest was that they had to run.

Some of that got through, since Een turned toward the door and staggered in that direction. Fighting panic, Serge got an arm around his waist where the *faiina* were beginning to soften again, and supported Een outside, down the steps, and into the truck. He managed to convey to Een that he needed to lie down on the front seat, out of sight, before he covered Een with a blanket. Then he rushed back inside to where the agents still sprawled all over his living room floor and hallway.

The white strings Een had shot out were already dissolving or evaporating, Serge wasn't certain which. He checked Agent Saunders first—still breathing— then the others. Whatever Een had done hadn't killed them, thank ever-loving fuck. Extremities started to twitch, and before Serge could come up with a viable plan, the agents were sitting up and opening dazed eyes. One by one, they got to hands and knees, shaking heads, letting out little moans, then each got to his or her feet.

Serge held both hands out in a placating gesture. "Look, I can explain—"

Agent Saunders wandered away from him, holstering her service weapon. She didn't seem aware of him yet and Serge stood silent, waiting. Running would've been more sensible, but this was all too bizarre and he'd feel wrong about abandoning people who were obviously disoriented and maybe suffering neurological damage.

Suddenly, Special Agent Saunders turned toward him and advanced, face set and grim as it had been before Een had made his appearance. "Please stand out of the way, Mr. Kosygin. We won't break your dishes or toss the drawers."

"I..." Serge watched open-mouthed as she marched into the now-empty guestroom. "Um, all right?"

"Curtis, take the other bedroom. Feldhauer, check under the house. Marshall, you keep an eye on Kosygin," she called out.

Sounds of rummaging in closets and under the front porch soon followed her orders. Serge stood in the middle of his living room with his arms wrapped tight around his ribs, trying not to shake. It was as if the moments before Een had done—whatever he had done—those moments were gone for the agents. Erased.

There wasn't much to search in a four-room cabin. Within ten minutes, the agents had reconvened around him.

"Anything?" Saunders barked out. Her colleagues shook their heads. "You live alone here, Kosygin?"

"I do now. My husband passed away recently."

Saunders frowned, though it didn't seem to be in disapproval. "Sorry to hear that. You use both beds."

Oh, the unmade bed in the guest room. "Not usually. Sometimes I have a friend stay over."

She nodded, still frowning. "All right. Thank you for your time, Mr. Kosygin. Sorry to bother you. Don't leave town, though. We may have additional questions."

"Of course." Completely flummoxed, Serge escorted them out of the house and saw them on their way.

As soon as they were out of sight, he dashed back inside and started stuffing clothes in a duffle bag. Duffle and laptop straps over his shoulder, he rushed out to the truck, barely remembering to snag wallet and keys along the way. There was no way this was the end of things. Those agents knew something was off, they'd realize something was *really* off about this last visit, and they'd be back. They'd keep coming back until they dragged Een away.

Een was still curled up under the blanket, as still as a terrified fawn, but he peeked out when Serge climbed into the cab.

"Who?"

Serge started the truck and backed onto the gravel drive before he answered. "Who were they? Government agents. The authorities. Sent by the people...damn it, I never know which words you've already learned."

"Law?" Een asked. "Broken?"

"No, I..." Serge hesitated. Had he broken any laws? He'd reported the crash, given aid to the one survivor, and despite what the agents had said he wasn't holding Een against his will. "No. We haven't broken any laws. But a lot of aliens, other species, have come here.

People this planet has never seen before. The government is worried, I guess. Wants to keep track. I'm not sure... Not sure if they'd hurt you."

Een nodded, though how much of that he'd picked up was unclear. When they reached the bottom of the hill, Serge took a breath and tried to restart his brain. What the hell was he doing? Where would they go? Motel. He'd get them a room in some nondescript little place, the kind where guests pulled up to the motel room door. There were people at the university, ones in the right departments who had been Josh's friends and colleagues. Once he had Een settled, he'd make some calls. He could still fix this. Have some help negotiating the situation. Make sure Een was safe.

"It'll be okay."

"Government humans? Hurt?"

"Did you hurt them?" Serge glanced over at Een huddled in his blanket against the passenger door. Even without human expressions, he managed to radiate misery. "No, they were fine. What did you do? With your *lim*? What was that?"

"*Melai*," Een sang, which answered nothing.

"*Melai*? The white strings that came from your *lim*? What did they do?"

Een shifted, his fingers reaching for a keyboard that wasn't there, so Serge knew he was struggling. "*Melai* stop movement. Human weapon at Serge."

"Mother of God," Serge muttered. "You have built in tasers. You were protecting me? Keeping me from getting hurt?"

"Yes. Weapons."

"Right. She pulled her gun. Scared you, huh?" Serge mulled that over as he pulled out sweats for Een and a long scarf to wrap around his head. "Does the *melai* make you forget things? Makes pieces of your memory go away?"

Een stopped pulling on the sweatpants to stare at him. "Forget? No. Stops moving."

"Guess human neurology's a little different from what you're used to. Those agents forgot that they saw you. They don't remember you."

Een finished dressing in silence as Serge turned onto the main road. He pulled the blanket back around him and curled up against the door again, staring at the floor and occasionally uttering single, plaintive chords.

CHAPTER SIX_

THE NEW DWELLING SEEMED A TEMPORARY SORT, more like a spaceport cabin than a place to call home. There were no facilities for Serjeh to prepare himself food, for one, and the single room offered no separation, something humans seemed to need.

Een didn't completely understand what had happened. Other humans, humans in authority, had arrived and had upset Serjeh. They had *frightened* him, then threatened him. Whether the other humans had meant harm or whether Serjeh merely thought so didn't seem important in that moment when the closest human had drawn a weapon. He couldn't stand by and watch his host, his friend, hurt for trying to protect him.

Perhaps panicking and throwing the *melai* hadn't been the best choice, but it was only supposed to keep them still until more reasonable thinking prevailed. The *melai* had paralyzed them, yes, but also rendered them unconscious and, according to Serjeh, had stolen bits of memory. He should have realized that reactions would be unpredictable with unfamiliar physiology.

He hadn't been thinking except to protect Serjeh. Perhaps he had committed a crime. It made him dizzy to think so, his joints aching from worry. Serjeh had been on his pocket communication device for some time, seeming more and more agitated as he paced and spoke. He had smiled for Een, said everything would be *okay*, and had left the temporary dwelling.

If only he'd had a little more time to understand this new world before having to face it. With no knowledge of social or governing structures, he was at a loss, anxious over how grave the situation actually was. What if Serjeh now felt he was too much of a risk? What if he had abandoned Een in this place? At least he had left the larger data device. Een tried to bury himself in language study, devouring concepts and context, wishing Serjeh was there to answer questions.

Serjeh would come back. He would. Een trusted him. *Liked* him. More than liked. He had never felt so comfortable and companionable with any other alien being. While the rational part of him said that he couldn't understand the motives of a being he could barely speak to, every fiber of his physical being said that Serjeh was just as he seemed—patient, gentle, and compassionate.

The first sharp aches in his *lim* surprised him as he struggled through information on *federal agents*. He dismissed it as the aftermath of throwing *melai*, something he hadn't had any need to do since he'd matured and taken mates. But the pain grew worse as he waited for Serjeh, and when he reached up to touch one of the *lim*, the outer covering was tender.

He had been expecting it, of course, just not so soon. It was probably for the best that this came now. Serjeh didn't deserve to be driven from his home, and with Een gone, he would be able to return to his life.

Serjeh returned before full dark with packages and furtive looks out their single small window. When it seemed he was satisfied with whatever the outside world had to show him, he turned to the packages and produced a lamp with the proper light spectrum for Een to feed and water in sealed containers.

"Een? Are you all right?"

"I am..." Een waved his fingers as the language implant processed. "Ill. Sick?"

Serjeh moved the lamp so it shone more fully on Een. "Does that help?"

"It is more." Een waited until Serjeh sat beside him and held his hand. His vocabulary grew each day, but he wasn't certain he could explain this with the words he had. He had to do his best for Serjeh, though. "Aalana...adult Aalana mate."

"Yes." Serjeh gazed at him in what seemed earnest concern. "Humans do that, too."

Een shook his head. He hadn't said it right. "Adult Aalana *must* mate."

The skin of Serjeh's forehead wrinkled, an odd expression that Een had been able to associate with puzzlement. "You have to mate or you get sick? What if you don't have a mate?"

"If other Aalana lived here...there are Aalana who help. With no mate. Their...job?"

Serjeh stroked his smooth thumb over the back of Een's hand. "So if you were home, there'd be other

Aalana whose job it is to, um, help out. If you didn't have a mate. What happens if you're alone?"

Een nodded, since Serjeh sounded as if he had put things together correctly. "Alone, we become sick." He waved a hand at his *lim*. "I pollinate. The *lim* do this. Without mates the pollen...stuck? Gathers. Swells."

Linguistically, he knew he was stumbling badly, hoping that throwing more words out would help.

Serjeh reached up and ran a finger gently over one of the outer *lim*. Even that careful touch was painful, but Een sat still, allowing his examination.

"Een, they're hot. Are they painful?"

"Yes."

"Can I get you some ice? Is there anything I can do?" Serjeh took both of his hands. "How does it get better?"

Too many questions, Een had trouble following. He would need to find *ice* in the database later. "It is bad fast. Surprising. I must pollinate."

"Or what? What happens if you can't?"

"I will die."

Serjeh drew in a sharp breath. "No. No, we can't let that happen. What can I do?"

"Do? Stay with me? I have...expected this."

With a little cry, Serjeh ran both hands through his hair. "You knew this was coming. And you didn't say anything. How can you be so calm?"

"What thing to do? There is nothing. No mates. No Aalana."

Serjeh got up to wander the room in sharp steps, as he did when upset or considering. "How do your mates help you pollinate? Could I help you? Why does it need to be another Aalana?"

"Do you pollinate without females?"

"I do. I always have." Serjeh took the data device from Een and placed it on the nearest surface. "I don't *need* to do it. But I've always done it with other males. Or by myself."

Een considered. He'd always been taught that the presence of the catalyst spores and the ova allowed pollination to occur. Perhaps...it could be done without? Though if that were true, surely other pollinators would have done so.

"Let me help you," Serjeh said in his softest, almost toneless voice as a drop of moisture leaked from his left eye.

They were such lovely eyes, so strange and dark, but so beautiful. Worried, Een caught the drop of moisture on his thumb. "You are injured? Your eye..."

"Those are tears, Een. They're normal. I'm fine. Our eyes use them to flush things out or they happen when we get upset."

"Upset?"

"I don't want you to die. Een, please. Let me try."

Despite the language barrier, Een understood what Serjeh intended. While it most likely wouldn't help his situation in any lasting way, a bit of physical comfort certainly couldn't hurt, and Serge seemed so unhappy. No, he wasn't being truthful with himself. He *wanted* Serjeh's touch. More than his lim yearned toward him. The harmony they had found together, such an unexpected connection, was bittersweet now that Een knew it would be so short. He didn't want Serjeh to suffer and he knew, again being truthful, that Serjeh would when he died. Whatever he could offer now, he offered with all his being and hoped it would help stave off the darkness.

"How?" Een asked as he curled up on the bed, facing Serjeh. "For you?"

Serjeh hesitated, then let out one of those gusty breaths. "No, no. This is about you, not me."

"Both," Een insisted and tried to imitate one of Serjeh's smiles. "You and I. Both."

"Hmm, okay, but—"

"You remove your coverings?" Een knew this to be the case since he had watched footage of humans mating. That had been a pollinator and an ovulator, male and female, though. Perhaps it was different for two pollinators.

"I...yeah. Sometimes," Serjeh said as he stared at the corner of the bed.

Een tugged at Serjeh's top covering. "Both. Mine removed. You."

"You took yours off the second we got in here. Fine. All right. If it makes you more comfortable."

The uncovering process fascinated Een. First Serjeh pulled the top covering off over his head, revealing a torso liberally sprinkled with human *faiina*. Hair. He had to remind himself to use human terms. This was quite different from the uncovered humans he had seen on the data device, who had been strangely smooth, like spacer textiles. Serjeh was far more attractive than those denuded specimens. Some of the hair was even the beautiful silver color that sparked through the dark strands atop Serge's head.

The bottom coverings came next, with extra layers for Serjeh's feet and from waist to mid-thigh. With his odd reproductive construction, Een understood how that made sense and apparently Serjeh's circulatory system often left his extremities cold, so the foot coverings were sensible as well. He was so different, and also so beautiful.

Een held out his hands in welcome, the invitation clear without stumbling over strange words, and Serge eased onto the bed beside him so they lay face to face.

"What do I do?"

"Touch." Een brought one of Serjeh's hands to his *lim*, stroking Serjeh's fingers over one of the painful, swollen tendrils. "Touch and touch. Careful. Soft."

"Okay. Gentle, I got it. Any one of them? All of them?"

Despite the pain, Een couldn't help a trill of pleasure at having his *lim* stroked so tenderly. It helped to some extent, though the *lim* reacted to Serjeh's touch, swelling further, leaving the casings feeling tight and strained. Still, it was wonderful to have Serjeh touch him in more than a comforting way.

"And you? Serjeh? How best to touch?"

"Um..." Serjeh glanced down where his reproductive organ stood out from his body, straight and engorged in the state Een had learned indicated arousal. But he seemed hesitant, uncomfortable. Serjeh had been mated. Surely this wasn't new for him. Maybe this was a human thing and there were traditional mating phrases and rituals Een was skipping past in his ignorance.

"Touch?" Een asked softly. "With fingers? Good?"

"Yeah." Serjeh's voice had an odd rasp to it. "Fingers are good. You don't have to be as gentle with me."

Een nestled closer and closed his dominant hand

around Serjeh's tube. The skin was warm and soft, a lovely, smooth column under his fingers. A long, low sound came from Serjeh as he pressed his forehead against Een's shoulder.

"Hurt?"

Serjeh huffed, a sound of amusement. "No, no... Een. That feels so good."

A ball of heated light lodged at Een's center at being able to bring pleasure. He hooked his leg over Serjeh's and pulled him closer, leaning into the hands caressing his *lim*. Some part of the terrible shadow of loneliness lifted in this simple joy of sharing physical space. Some light warmed him in being able to please someone he cared about. There would be no relief from it, not for him. That frustrating blocked feeling throbbed in his *lim*, the one he had only experienced previously in times of stress when he could not pollinate. Even so, Serjeh's touch was wonderful.

He moved his fingers up and down Serjeh's shaft as he had observed the humans in the data vids do, tugging gently, and running the pad of his thumb across the tip.

"Harder...please." Serjeh's breaths came shorter, sharper.

Een did his best and there were frustrated growls and several adjustments. Soon though, Serjeh's hands stilled in Een's *lim*, his hips twitching and jerking in time to Een's tugs. A warm, earthen scent filled the air. Then heated ropes of white shot from the tip of Serjeh's pollinator. This had been shocking the first time Een had seen it on the vids, thinking it was a neurotoxin like the *melai* from an Aalana's *lim*. But it was merely the delivery method used for the human pollinator gametes. It was sticky, but pleasantly so, and Serjeh calmed quickly after his release, removing Een's hand gently.

"Are you even close?" Serjeh whispered, moving a hand to stroke Een's face.

"No. It will not." Een folded Serjeh in his arms, crooning softly. "It was good. Thank you, Serjeh. My harmonies with yours. My Serjeh. But I...can't."

"God, Een...I'm sorry." Serjeh did an odd thing. He leaned in and brushed his mouth over Een's. The touch was tender and most likely meant as a comfort, though it was strange for Een. "What can I do?"

"Stay with me. There is nothing else. I am last. I will die."

The water gathered in Serjeh's eyes again and Een regretted his words. But it was true. He couldn't hide the truth. This way they were both prepared. Serjeh was with him and he needn't be afraid of facing his end alone.

———

SERGE TRIED to keep his frantic brain from spinning. He sat on the end of the bed with his head in his hands, Een's feet in his lap. After their unsuccessful attempt at getting Een to pollinate, Een had fallen asleep. Attempts to wake him fully after that failed. Serge could get him to drink some water, though he usually drank through his damn *lim*, too, and wasn't getting much anymore, but beyond that groggy half-awareness, Een didn't come around. His beautiful lavender coloring had faded to a dull heather. All his *lim* were fever-hot while the rest of his body was cold, even when Serge put him directly under the sun lamp.

No one from the university had returned his calls. He hadn't gone so far as to say, *help, my alien friend is dying,* but he'd thought of the colleagues he'd contacted as friends. Asking for help should have gotten him some response. Nothing. Not a whisper.

Going into the office to find someone to talk to face to face hadn't seemed a viable option. He couldn't leave Een, especially not when he'd promised to stay with him. Hours were slipping away, hours Een didn't have. Fucking universe. He wasn't going to just sit here and watch someone else he cared about slip away, was he? No. Not again. Not so soon. No.

Morning slid in under the door, and he couldn't stand it any longer. Someone was going to talk to him. Someone was going to promise not to hand Een over to the government and someone was going to try to save him. *Yes. Fuck you death. Fuck you. You can't have Een.*

As carefully as he could, Serge bundled Een's long frame back into his borrowed sweats and socks. The sleeves and the legs were too short. He couldn't even think about pulling the hood up over Een's swollen *lim* and wrapping the scarf around his head made him gasp and moan in pain.

"Hey." Serge put a hand to the side of Een's face, pleased when his eyes slid half open. "We're going for a drive. When we get there, I might have to leave you in the truck for a few minutes. But it won't be long, okay?"

One corner of Een's mouth exhibited the smallest curl upward. "Okay."

The notes were so faded, barely audible. Serge packed their little bit of luggage behind the front seat, wrapped Een in the blanket from the truck, and set him gently in the passenger seat. A quick checkout and they were on the road, Een curled up on bench seat with his head in Serge's lap. At least he didn't have to worry about anyone spotting Een as they drove. The federal agents might not be looking for them yet, but he had the feeling that was just a matter of time. Someone was going to figure out that they had more questions for Serge and that he'd abandoned his cabin. He wasn't even sure if he'd locked the door, which would look bad if he hadn't.

The drive to the Pitt campus should have been so familiar, but he felt strangely disconnected, as if seeing the students and the buildings through Een's eyes. Humans were strange creatures when he thought about them too hard, and so many of the glass and concrete buildings struck him as ugly. He parked in the garage by the Medical Arts building, nestled into a far, dark corner.

"Een." He lifted a corner of the blanket to stroke Een's *lim*. "Tell me you'll be all right if I leave you here."

"Serjeh?" The wavering notes, uneven and broken, broke Serge's heart. "You will come?"

"Will I come back? Of course I will. I'll hurry back as fast as I can."

"I will wait."

That was the best Serge could hope for, that Een would hang on until he returned. There was no question of decorum or respectful behavior. Serge ran. Full out, for all he was worth, shouting *sorry* when he bumped someone, not daring to take the time to look back. When he reached the correct floor and the correct department admin, he clutched at her desk, gasping.

"Mr. Kosygin?"

"Donna—" He held up a finger to ask for a moment and gulped a breath. "Is Dr. Carver in today? Dr. Phillips? Dr. Ahmal?"

Donna's raised eyebrow was her only sign of surprise. "Dr. Ahmal is on vacation for the week. Dr. Carver is visiting up at SUNY Albany. And Dr. Phillips is with a class."

That explained why he hadn't heard back from Omar or Greg. "Can you page him? I—it's an emergency."

"Mr. Kosygin, if you have a medical emergency, you should head to the ER, don't you think?"

"It's not— Please, Donna. I need help. Kurt's the only one here who might have a chance of understanding."

She shook her head. "I'll message him because you look about three sharp words from a complete breakdown, but I can't make promises. Please have a seat. You're making me jittery, looming like that."

"Yes, ma'am," Serge said miserably and sank into the chair by the door. He would've preferred Omar, who had been Josh's friend and sort of Serge's, too, someone who had actually been out to the house and called sometimes to see that Serge hadn't simply died without his husband. He only knew Kurt Phillips from social functions. What if he didn't take it seriously? What if he didn't come? What if he decided it was all too risky and he called the feds?

Donna looked up from her screen. "He's coming, but he says you'd better be on fire."

"I can arrange that if it helps." Serge shot up from the chair. "Ask him to meet me by the ground floor elevator in the parking garage. Please."

"Fine. Your funeral, professor. He already sounds annoyed."

"He's always annoyed. Just please ask him. I'll be down there." Serge hurried off, remembering to call over his shoulder, "Thank you! So much!"

Serge ran back to the garage and paced by the elevators, his heart slamming against his sternum. Speech after explanation speech played in his head, but he knew when it came to actually speaking, he was just going to blurt shit out the way he always did.

Maybe five minutes had passed when the elevator doors opened on Kurt's bland Anglo face and his sharp voice. "Completely inappropriate, Serge, interrupting my class. If this is some personal, existential crisis, I sw—"

"No. Kurt, listen. I have an alien in my truck. He's dying. The alien. Een's been staying with me but now he's sick and he says he's dying. Help. I need help."

"Perfect. Now you've lost your mind. I'm calling campus security."

"No! Just come with me." Serge tugged on his lab coat sleeve, relieved when Kurt actually followed. "I rescued Een from a crash site. He was doing so well until this. And I don't know how to fix it. He can't die. Please."

Kurt huffed and muttered all the way to the truck, but fell silent once Serge opened the door and lifted the blanket to show him Een. "Serge...you know I have to contact the FBI about this. He's not registered, is he?"

"They came to the cabin and wanted to take him away. You can't let them do that." Serge put a protective hand on Een's shoulder. "They'll lock him away and he'll die while they try to understand him."

"I can't—"

"You have the other Aalana here. His companions who died in the crash. It's not any secret Pitt got the bodies for study. You have to know something about them by now. Help me!"

"Serjeh?" Een woke, reaching for him with a trembling hand. "Who?"

"A friend," Serge reassured him as he gathered Een's long frame into his arms. He seemed to have lost weight in the time it took to drive from the motel. "A person I hope can help you."

"Friend," Een whispered the word as a wavering chord as he rested his head on Serge's shoulder.

Kurt stared at them with a dark frown for an agonizing moment. Then he turned and strode away, Serge's heart plummeting until Kurt said, "Hurry up, then. Let's get him into a patient room. I need to make some calls."

"Not the feds, please don't!"

"Stop being so dramatic. The feds. You're in a crime drama now?" Kurt snorted as he pulled his phone from his pocket. "We've done preliminary work on the bodies, but only as far as basic physiological structure. Tell me, briefly, what you know about him. What he eats, how much he communicates and so on."

"He...he doesn't eat." Serge put his back against the elevator wall and adjusted Een more comfortably in his arms. Briefly? "He's a plant."

"Why do you say that?"

"He doesn't eat anything, but he needs sunlight for fuel. Photosynthesis or whatever he does. When he first started learning our language, he started with Josh's wildflower guide. It...attracted him. And he referred to males as *pollinators*."

"Does he need water?"

"Oh, yes. He does. Though he's refused to take any today."

"A sentient plant," Kurt mused as he scrolled through his contacts and tapped in a call. "Absolutely amazing. Elena? It's Kurt Phillips. Whatever you're doing, drop it. I need you to come over to Medical Arts. What was that? Oh, no. Much better than dead aliens."

Kurt repeated the process with someone named Kevin before he bothered to explain. "Elena Frank from Biology and Kevin Vitelli, very sharp post-grad over in Bioengineering. You're lucky I've already started putting a team together."

"Yeah, okay. I know Elena," Serge rasped out and cleared his throat. No crying. Not now. Elena had at least been a colleague of Josh's. She did more cellular-level botany, but it was still botany.

"Biology," Een murmured into the side of Serge's throat. "Life."

"Yes, the study of life." Serge tried to sound upbeat even though his voice cracked. "When did you pick that word up?"

But Een had drifted off again, only uttering soft trills of pain whenever Serge moved. They hurried through the corridors, collecting some odd looks, but Een was covered up again and most people in the medical building were too busy for curiosity. At the end of a quieter corridor, Kurt waved them into a room with the usual monitoring equipment and a hospital bed. Kurt must have paged the nurses' station since a nurse with magenta hair and a bright pixie face soon joined them.

"Hi, I'm Sam," she bustled over with a smile and a sunlamp. "And this is Een, is that right?"

"He's, um..." Serge had to swallow hard. "He might not answer right now. But yeah, this is Een."

"Are you related?" She shook her head when Serge gaped. "Sorry. Bad joke. But you're his partner, Serge, yes?"

"I'm..." Serge was going to say no. What came out was a ragged, "Yeah."

"Great. You get to stay. Any idea what normal temp is for Een?" She elevated the head of Een's bed and set the sunlamp up so it shone directly on him.

SERGE SHOOK HIS HEAD MISERABLY. "I'm sorry. He's, um, colder at night and warmer during the day, usually."

"Okay. You're doing fine, Serge." She took a forehead thermometer out of her pocket and took a reading. "Just for a baseline. Any orders, Dr. Phillips?"

Kurt leaned against the counter out of the way. "Not yet."

Another bustle out and in, and Sam returned with water and extra blankets, which she tucked around Een. "How does Een usually drink?"

"Through his lim," Serge hitched a breath and waved at them. "The tube appendages on his head. But they're too swollen. Sometimes...that first night...he drank using his mouth. I guess when he's not doing so well."

She checked the *lim* visually and nodded, then held the glass in front of Een. "Can you drink for me, Een?"

Two soft chords answered her, but Een didn't seem able to lift his head even that far. She nodded again and produced a straw from her pockets of holding from which she stripped the paper cover and offered the glass again. Now Een could get his mouth around the straw and get some water down.

Why didn't I think of a straw?

The eerie quiet in the patient room disturbed Serge until he realized it was because there weren't any machines beeping or pinging. There was always beeping and pinging. Kurt stayed against the counter by the sink, silent and brooding, and only came to life when Dr. Frank and Kevin arrived.

Serge's vision blurred at the sight of a more welcoming face. "Elena?"

"Oh, Serge." She hurried over to offer a quick hug. "They didn't tell me you were involved. But I should've put it together. You sit. We have questions."

"Okay." Serge pulled in a few deep breaths. "I'll do my best."

"Kurt texted the basics. That Een's more of a plant analogue than animal. Why do you think he's dying?"

"It's his *lim*. I mean what's happening to them."

"The *lim* are the structures on his head?" Kevin asked without looking up from his tablet.

"Right. They're stuck. I mean, um, blocked. He's a pollinator and they're blocked."

Elena examined the length of one and peered into

the opening, but didn't touch. "That's the function of the *lim*? Pollen production?"

"One of them. They also have a natural defense thing they can do called *melai* and I think Een uses them as kind of an extra sense of smell, too."

Now Kevin looked up. "But it's not the *melai* causing the issue?"

"No. Definitely the pollen. He can't mate without mates." Serge dragged both hands over his face. "*God*. I mean, he can't pollinate without other adult Aalana. And if he can't, it blocks the *lim*. The pollen. And the blockage is killing him."

Elena put a hand on his arm. "So Een needs an adult female? Pistil to his stamen?"

"No, no, it's more complicated than that. Female, yes, but they both need another gender we don't have. They're sort of—"

"Three genders, then?" Elena interrupted him.

"Yes. For reproduction. I don't know, maybe they have more, but three for a mating group," Serge scrubbed his hands over his face again, perilously close to tears. "His two mates were the ones who died in their pod crash. Without them, it doesn't work."

"Een," Elena touched his shoulder. "Can you answer some questions for us?"

He didn't respond until Serge perched on the edge of the bed and sang one of the notes of his name chord, "Een."

"You are still here," Een whispered. "Good."

"These people are here to help." Serge took his hand since Een always responded better to communication accompanying touch. "Can you try to answer some things?"

"Sing?"

"I didn't bring the lute. I'm sorry. But I'll sing to you after they ask you things, okay?"

"Okay." Een squeezed his hand, making it clear Serge wasn't allowed to let go.

Elena pulled up a rolling stool and asked her questions slowly and patiently, sometimes repeating things another way if Een appeared confused. She would have been a better candidate for medical doctor than sharp-as-glass Kurt.

Een told her, as best he could, about the missing two genders, the one who provided the seed, the female, and the other who provided what sounded like spores, the one who had no human equivalent. All three partners had to be present and the pollinator actually acted as the receiver. Whatever the result was, a cocoon or an egg or something, Een didn't quite have the vocabulary to explain it, ended up forming on the pollinator's chest.

A few more questions about the ova producer and the spore producer and Kevin looked up from his tablet where he had been taking notes at a furious rate. "It might be possible. Everything's remained frozen. If not, we may be able to reverse engineer the process at least chemically?"

He wandered off with Kurt, both of them muttering over the notes. Elena patted Een's shoulder as she got to her feet. "We have some work to do. Een, your only job is to rest, all right?"

"Okay," Een whispered, the notes in his voice no more than brush strokes on a drum.

Left alone, Serge had little to do but worry. He helped Een out of his borrowed sweatshirt to give him more light exposure and made a sort of nest out of blankets and pillows so Een could rest his poor swollen *lim* a little more comfortably. He sang as he'd promised, his voice steadying after the first quavering notes while Een hummed in accompaniment. After a *Kyrie*, a modified *In Natali*, and a shortened rendition of *Greensleeves*, Een drifted back to sleep and Serge stretched out beside him, hoping his body warmth might help.

How long they were alone with the sounds of ventilation and Serge's breathing their only company, he couldn't have said. No clock, no watch, nothing but anxiety making the time stretch out interminably. When Een twitched and tossed restlessly, Serge stroked his *faiina* until they softened and lay flat again. All the hours together, sharing notes, pouring over wildflowers, trading bits of language and dance—all the quiet, small things they had together, those had driven this change. Serge had slid from simply concerned, from feeling responsible for another life, to caring deeply for Een, this gentle, curious soul. A tiny light had caught in the ashes of Serge's heart, fed day by day with little twigs of mutual need.

If Een died, that light would go out. The roiling, clinging mists he'd been lost in since Josh's death would come rushing back and Serge was sure he wouldn't find his way out again. He wasn't sure he wanted to try.

"Stay, Een," he whispered. "Please stay. Just a little longer. Please."

THE LIGHTS WERE TOO BRIGHT. EEN'S BODY TOLD him it was night and Serjeh's dwelling should have been pleasantly dim by now. Serjeh was beside him, his arm wrapped over Een's chest, his scent comforting and familiar. But everything else was wrong. Steel and antiseptic, this room smelled more like a space station. Had they taken a shuttle off-planet? No. That didn't sound right.

Humans moved about the room, purposeful, nearly silent, the purpose of their hurried movements a mystery. One of them was familiar. He remembered that one. Her? Did he recall Serjeh speaking of this person using the female pronoun? Yes. Her. Dr. Franks. She had spoken to him about the mechanics of mating. A scientist, he was certain. He was happy to discuss differences in reproductive biology...

Wait, no. Serjeh had brought him to a medical facility. Dr. Franks was trying to discover a way to save him. He remembered. But remembering was so difficult.

Serjeh sat up beside him now, speaking softly. Struggling to focus on his words, Een lifted a hand to stroke Serjeh's face. "Slow. I don't understand."

"Dr. Franks has...this is hard to say." Serjeh closed his eyes tight. They were wet when he reopened them. "Your mates, their bodies are here in this building. They were frozen. Preserved, right? Dr. Franks hopes they've been able to get the right...parts for you. The seed, I guess. And the...the spores. So with them you can pollinate. Maybe."

Een hummed a bit, thinking that over. He wished his Aal and his Laiin were there to hold him. Then he could. Without hesitation. Perhaps, though, just perhaps, he could do this last thing for them. Mate one last time in absentia, without chemical prophylactic interference that would prevent the gametes from joining.

"I will try."

"That's all we can ask." Serjeh performed that odd ritual where he touched his mouth to Een's, but this time it was comforting. Simply another way Serjeh showed how he cared. "They're going to put both on your chest. I know that can't be quite...right. I'll help you any way I can."

"I know. Serjeh. Lie down with me."

No, it wasn't right. Laiin should be nestled close on one side, Aal on the other, stroking him, nuzzling at him. Aal's pleasure came first, as was proper. His spores were the catalyst to release Laiin's seed, and ultimately, Een's pollen. Serge lay beside him, at least. Though his body was too warm and smooth, his hands were gentle and soothed some of Een's worry.

"The spores first, Een?" Dr. Franks was asking. She

might have said it more than once. It was difficult to concentrate through the pain.

"Yes. Aal. His name was Aal. His spores." Een moved Serjeh's hand up from his chest. "Serjeh, like before. What we did."

Serjeh understood and began stroking the tender *lim*, nestling closer when Een slid an arm around him. With gloved hands, Dr. Franks placed a cake of some organic substance on his chest, and from the scent it was saturated with Aal's spores. Een's *lim* waved and yearned toward it, picking up the particulates, the uniquely flavored molecules that had been Aal, his bright, clever Aal.

"That's it," Serjeh encouraged softly. "You can do this."

Keening notes rose from Een's throat, mourning his mate even as he reveled in this strange, disjointed reunion. Then, oh, then, Dr. Franks placed the seed on his chest, the scent opening a flood of memories, of Laiin, fearless and strong, who had kept them safe, who had led them through every crisis. Laiin...Laiin and Aal. His every cell cried out for them in desperate longing, his need so great he felt as if he might fly apart. But then Serjeh moved closer, his scent mingling with those Een had lost. Serjeh, Serjeh, holding him here, striving to keep Een together. His need for Serjeh was just as great, major cadences soothing over the minor.

"I've got you," Serjeh whispered, both hands stroking his *lim*. "I've got you. Let go, Een. It'll be all right now."

The need rose to a shriek, his *lim* stiffening, all pointing down toward his chest. He cried out, in agony, in pleasure, in a devastating mingling of grief and joy. His *lim* released their pollen in sticky violet strings, raining down on his chest to cover both Laiin's seed and Aal's spore cake, mingling the three as they were meant to.

He knew he whimpered, fading in and out of consciousness, Serjeh still beside him, murmuring comforting words, his line back to the light. Couldn't sleep. Not yet.

"Serjeh, help me," Een whispered, gesturing that he wanted to sit up to see. It seemed too much to hope for but, yes, the gametes were bonding, forming the pod as his pollen hardened around the seed. "It needs...I need..."

"What do we need to do?" Serjeh asked, pointing to the pod. "The...is this an Aalana young person now?"

"Water. For young." Een tried for words. "To...to be in."

"We need a container? With water for it to float in?"

Een nodded and lay back again, exhausted. "It... germinates now." He recalled that word from reading about the holly's reproduction. "Please. It must be soon."

With swift gestures, Dr. Franks sent younger humans scurrying and one brought a container of water with room for the pod to grow and a lid with regularly spaced circular openings. Whether this planet's water was suitable or not, Een had no way to know. But he couldn't simply let the youngling die, the only youngling he and Aal and Laiin would ever have since Een was certain he wouldn't survive the night. Serjeh helped him since his hands shook so badly and together they secured the pod within the container, floating just beneath the surface, confirmation that the pod was viable. If it had sunk like a stone, any hope of it developing would have been crushed. The youngling would require mineral supplements and light, and he told Serjeh so, but for now, it was safe.

"Thank you," he murmured to Serjeh. "Thank you. I am...tired."

Serjeh smiled for him. "Go to sleep, then. I'll be here. Me and the baby."

CHAPTER EIGHT_

Elena pulled Serge out into the hallway after Een had been asleep for an hour. "I know what you said to Kurt, but listen, You have to let us call the OAA."

"What? No." Serge yanked his arm free. "Hell no. *Fuck* no. All those aliens that've landed in this country —no one ever sees them again. That is *not* happening to Een."

"Serge," she frowned up at him. "What in the world do you think is happening to them?"

"They're being held in some lab." Serge waved his arms, not so much gesticulating as beating the air. "Tortured. Dissected. Interrogated. How the hell would I know? But they land and they vanish."

She rubbed at her forehead. "I can see where that might come from. They haven't vanished. Their privacy is carefully protected so the press doesn't hound them or whackos who might wish them harm. The OAA places aliens with host families, helps them with resettling. Serge, there are procedures in place.

Good ones. And lots and lots of paperwork. This isn't the X-Files."

"But they came to the house. Threatened me. Scared the hell out of Een."

"Because..." She poked a finger at his chest. "They thought you'd hidden an alien body. They didn't know Een was alive. They thought you were some kind of ghoulish weirdo."

"Oh. Um...oh."

"We're calling them. They can help with things like funding and with other alien contacts if Een wants to talk to any of the others. Not to mention, protecting both of you from actual weirdos."

Serge drooped against the corridor wall. "Fine. All right. But Een stays here in the Medical Arts Building. These agents don't move him anywhere. And he doesn't get left alone with them."

"I think we can convince them." She pointed to Een's door. "Stay with him. Sit tight."

Maybe, just maybe, he'd been more paranoid than he had to be, but the newscasts could have said instead of keeping everything so hush-hush. Though maybe that would've just encouraged weirdos.

"I'm not a weirdo," Serge muttered as he settled next to Een's bed again.

"You are kind of a weirdo," Kurt said from the counter where he was reading something on his phone, damn him for being so quiet. "But a benign one. When Een's feeling up to it, we'd love to have his input on Aalana physiology."

"I'll ask him. When he's not sleeping off near death."

Kurt gave him what might have been his version of

a smile, a swift one-sided thing, and walked out without another word.

"That man's a jerk, Een." Serge scowled at the closed door. "But he helped save you. So I guess he's not as big a jerk."

Een hummed a chord in his sleep and Serge smiled down at him, so relieved he felt like he'd gone over a cliff and miraculously survived. He held Een's hand and settled with his arm on the mattress to wait.

He jerked up when the door opened again, stiff and headachy, realizing he'd fallen asleep leaning toward Een. Elena and Kurt had returned with Sam and another nurse, and already Elena was making little *stay calm* motions with her hands.

"They're here. Try to keep an open mind, Serge."

Was he growling? He was and did his best to stop as Een woke to all the people in his room.

"Serjeh?"

"I'm here." He gripped Een's hand tighter. "Right here. There are people who want to talk to you. You feel up to it?"

"Up?" Een's notes were puzzled. "I lie down."

"Do you feel awake enough? Well enough?"

Een blinked a few times. "Yes. I can answer. For Dr. Franks?"

"No, um, it's—"

Agents in suits suddenly pushed into the room. Familiar agents. "Kosygin."

Serge tried for a civil tone. "Agent Sanders."

"Saunders." She pinched the bridge of her nose between thumb and forefinger. "You're doing that on purpose."

"Maybe."

She fixed him with her most piercing stare. "Mr. Kosygin, you're going to have to leave the room."

"Like hell I will."

"It's not a request." Saunders motioned to the two largest agents behind her and they surged forward to pin Serge's arms and frog march him to the door.

"Serjeh!"

His heart cracked at the anguish in Een's cry. "I'll be back. It's okay, Een! Elena, don't you leave him. Don't you let these fuckers take him. You promised! Don't leave him!"

Kurt snorted. "Drama queen."

Elena smacked his arm. "We'll be right here. Go sit in the hall for a bit. Everything's fine, Een. Serge will be just outside the door."

As promised, they remained. The two bruiser agents pulled up chairs and sat with Serge, their backs to the wall.

When Serge stopped struggling, the larger one, the one with the surprisingly soft voice spoke. "It's procedure, Mr. Kosygin. We have to be sure."

"Sure of *what?*"

"That Een's not being coerced or threatened by you."

"*What?*"

"Look. I think he's attached to you. That he has strong feelings about you. Not hard to see. But we need to make sure. This is for Een's safety and his well-being. Understand?"

Serge shifted in his chair, still furious, still shredding his heart with worry. "Maybe. I guess. You do this for all the landing immigrants?"

"Yes. Normally, host families are carefully vetted

and screened. We do check-in visits every month. That's our job, Mr. Kosygin. To make sure the aliens aren't exploited or harmed while they try to adjust to life here."

He didn't like being wrong and it made him squirm inside to think that maybe he had been. "Wait. What? Normally?"

"Yes." Soft Voice said with a little smile that was suspiciously smug.

The door to Een's room flew open and Agent Saunders stepped out, her face set in stone. She pointed an accusing finger at Serge. "You. Do you love him?"

Serge gaped at her. "What?"

Soft Voice murmured, "He says that a lot."

"You heard me," Saunders persisted. "Do. You. Love. Een?"

Do I? Serge poked at his battered heart where warmth had started to gather, where sparks had started to catch fire. Every bit of that new heat sang the same notes—*Een, Een, Een.* He met her gaze and surprised himself by saying out loud what he hadn't admitted to himself. "Yes. I love Een."

She covered her face and sighed into her hands before lowering them again. "Let him back in the room. We don't have procedures for this. They're in love. They just made a baby. They're going to be parents."

"Every day's a new world in this job, Marina." Soft Voice helped Serge up onto shaking legs. "Congratulations, Mr. Kosygin."

"Thank you?"

Serge wobbled into the room where Een held out his arms and sang his name and everyone, even Kurt, smiled to see it. He managed to make it to the bed without stumbling too much, Een's *lim* reaching for him as he plunked onto the mattress.

"Serjeh, you are cold," Een crooned as he folded Serge against him.

"I was scared for you." Serge put his head on Een's shoulder, letting his *lim* map Serge's face.

"Better?"

"Now, yeah. And you look better, too. You're almost the right color again." He stroked a finger along Een's jaw. "Still tired, though, I bet."

"Better. Tired." Een trilled and held him tighter. "I say stay with Serjeh. They say good."

"Great. We're all happy that you're not dead, Een, and that Kosygin isn't some alien necrophiliac." Saunders produced a briefcase from beside the door and started pulling out sheaves of paper. "It's all a little unorthodox and backward, but since domicile's been established by Een's request." She approached with the imposing pile. "You've got some forms to fill out."

Serge sat up, bemused and alarmed all over again, as Sam brought him a clipboard and a pen. "What... kind of forms?"

"This is your application for hosting an alien immigrant. This packet's a possible needs survey covering both physical and educational limitations. Financial statement. Medical history. These are the letters of reference we'll need to complete the application." Saunders turned over one stapled packet after another. "Your application for alien viability grant funds—"

"Grant...funds?" Serge squeaked as he forced the words out.

"Yes. We find most of our visitors need special accommodations to live with humans comfortably. Pools. Nests. Ramps for stairs. Planned renovations need to be approved, of course, but you need the application on file first."

Beside him, Een trilled, the notes vibrating through Serge's hip where he leaned against Een. "Are you *laughing* at me?"

"Humor. Yes." Een's next trill was muted as if he were trying to stifle it. "Your face. Someone gave you a—"

Whatever Aalana word Een sang, it probably meant something more along the lines of *a poisonous snake* rather than *a cute puppy*, and everyone insisted he fill out the forms right then while they waited for Een to be rested enough to go home. Not even the excuse of having left his reading glasses at home saved him. Sam brought him a magnifying glass.

"Right." Serge grumped as he started on the application. "Not the X-Files. They don't have paperwork."

Halfway through the fourth page of the application, he stopped, pen hovering over the page. "Een? I have to list the baby, the podling, whatever we're calling them. Do you have a name? For the baby?"

Een scooted closer, humming to himself, his silver eyes wandering. For a few seconds, Serge thought maybe Een hadn't understood the question. Then his gaze snapped over to Serge's face. "Naim."

"That's the baby's name? Naim?"

"Yes. Naim is..." Een's fingers waved a moment as

he searched for words. "The songs from stars." Een's trill was sleepy. "Soon with us. Eating stars."

Naim, Serge wrote in the space for primary immigrant's family. He'd have to remember to ask Een how long gestation was. He had a lot of work to do. With a put-upon sigh, he turned the packet over. *One form down.*

———

MARINA CAME with them to the dwelling. The *cabin.* He had learned that word today while she asked Serjeh questions about his home. Apparently, questions were not sufficient, and the government people had followed Serjeh's vehicle home. Partly, this was good. Their vehicle was better equipped to transport Naim's natal tank and Serjeh had help getting it up the steps.

Partly, it was not good. Serjeh was so tired, physically and socially.

His voice was brittle and sharp as he directed the other humans. "No, no, no. Not back in the bedrooms. Naim needs to be out *here.* Where there's more *light.* Are you trying to kill the baby?"

"Serjeh. They do not." Een stroked his arm. "Helping."

"Right. Helping. Sorry." Serjeh ran a hand over his face. "You should rest. Do you want to go to your room where it'll be quieter?"

"I will stay. Star...*sun* still gives light."

He settled on the window seat, out of the way of humans tramping this way and that with their heavy foot coverings. Resting beside Naim's birthing tank, listening to Serjeh and Marina argue about ways to change the cabin for *more light* and *infant safety*, it was enough.

His talk with Marina at the medical facility had made some things clear to him, though. His harmonies had matched with Serjeh's, without question, but he hadn't gone about this correctly at all. Circumstances would have made that difficult even with fully mindful intentions, of course.

Now that he would not only live but also thrive, it was time to take care of omissions.

CHAPTER NINE_

When Een woke two mornings later, he realized he must have fallen asleep on the window seat the evening before again and been unaware of anything after that. Serjeh had tucked Een under the blankets on his guest sleeping platform. This disappointed him a bit since he thought surely now Serjeh would want to share a platform, but perhaps this was correct for humans as well. There had been no courtship, no declarations beyond those purely of emotion. At least this morning he felt strong enough to rise and begin his day without assistance.

Across the hall, Serjeh's door stood open a crack, his sleeping form visible in the gathering light. Een's lim warmed at the sight of Serjeh sprawled on his back with one arm trailing over the edge of the platform. He hurried quietly past before distraction could end his resolve.

On a space station, Aalana had to find artificial substitutes, like grommets or colored *dipa* blocks. Laiin had taken an old data device apart and used the components. But here on a planet's surface, Een could use a more ancient, traditional item: small stones. Water vapor in the air—Een wasn't certain whether this was properly fog or mist—added a chill, but the sun would be visible soon, and wasn't that perfect? He could have sun-warmed stones just like in the old songs.

Nestled amid all the small people Serjeh referred to as *grass* and *wildflowers*, Een found an infinite variety of stones. He only took ones larger than his thumb, but still comfortable in his hand, making certain he had a variety of shades and patterns, some with striations or speckles, some with sparkling mineral intrusions, some a single color.

He gathered his mound on the porch and began placing the stones in a pattern to represent different wavelengths of light. This was not traditional, but a thing he felt had drawn him and Serjeh together. The last stone in place, he had just stepped back to check his pattern when Serjeh wandered out in nothing but the bottom half of pajamas. Een particularly liked the word *pajamas*. It had a warm and comfortable sound.

"Hey. How're you feeling?" Serjeh wrapped warm arms around him and leaned his head on Een's shoulder.

"I am well. Better."

"Good, good. What are you doing out here so early?"

Een waved to his pattern. "I have made you a *munalid*."

"For me?" Serjeh stepped closer to inspect the pattern more closely. "Why do I get the feeling this isn't just something pretty? Is this for something special?"

"It is..." Een wished he had brought the data pad out with him. "I am not certain of words. Dating? Courtship? Serenading?"

Red spots colored Serjeh's face, a sign of a strong emotional response. Een hoped it was a positive one. "A courtship ritual? How serious is this?"

Een wasn't sure he understood what the question meant, though he conceded that the *munalid's* significance was not something Serjeh would know yet. "It is... When Aalana choose mates, the *munalid* is first. I say with this, *my harmonies yearn toward yours.*"

"I see." Serjeh nodded, though the red coloration had only deepened. "So, um, let's say the person you've picked is interested, too. What do they do next?"

"That person looks. For meaning. For...pleasing?" Een let out a nervous trill, suddenly uncertain of himself, his words, and this course of action. "If...that person...if they also feel this, they...pattern answer?"

Still Serjeh nodded, no laughter or revulsion in his expression. "I think I get it. So if I want to court you back, I have to think about your pattern. It looks like waveforms and that could be light or sound. Light and music got us to start trying to communicate, so that makes sense." His arm around Een squeezed tight. "It's beautiful. I love it. Een, you already know I love you, right?"

"Yes." The word meant so many things, but the way Serjeh meant he had demonstrated many times, risking himself, giving of himself, all for Een. "I do. Also. Love you."

Now Serjeh smiled, though a drop of moisture still

slid from one eye. "Okay. That's...I feel like I'm negative a hundred pounds right now."

That made no sense, but Een would parse the phrasing later. "You accept my pattern?"

Serjeh pressed his mouth to Een's cheek. He knew now that it was a *kiss*, a sign of affection or passion or both. "Yes. It's wonderful. Do I do something now?"

"You..." Een should have tried to find words *before* he started this. The thought only flustered him more and only Aalana words came out first. Finally he tried, "You pattern back? If...if you...mating..."

"I think I get it." Serge took both Een's hands and pressed them to his chest. "If I also want you as my mate, I make a pattern now. Do I use your stones?"

Een nodded, too overcome to speak. He waved to the stones, to himself, to the front door and Serjeh laughed softly.

"All right. I'll figure out the stones while you go find some new words."

To his shame, he fled. There was no other word for his hasty, stumbling retreat into the house. If asked, Een wouldn't have been able to articulate why he was so nervous, but the *rah* thumped in his circulatory channels and his breaths whistled. Normally, a third person would be involved, of course. Perhaps that was why the *munalid's* significance loomed so large—the lack of a third to confer with or commiserate with.

Laptop open, settled into the patch of light on the floor in the front room, Een dove back into the rather confusing subject of human courtship and something called *marriage*.

· · ·

THE LIGHT HAD MOVED a few inches across the floor, and Een had moved with it, before Serjeh's shadow fell across him from the doorway. He still wore a little smile, his voice soft and tentative as he reached out a hand.

"I'm all set. You want to see?" A fine tremor ran through Serjeh's hand. At least he was nervous, too.

"Yes."

They stepped out into the sunlight and excitement swept Een's anxious thoughts away. Serjeh's pattern was so *interesting*. Two nearly identical patterns faced each other, each comprised of curling lines that diverged from a single point, the curls fanning out toward the pattern opposite. On one side, Serjeh had used the lighter stones and on the other, the darker ones. Een tipped his head to the side. He thought Serjeh had gathered extra stones, too, probably needing more to create such a large pattern.

Serjeh knelt and pulled Een down beside him. "So what do you think?"

What could it mean? If Een had brought out the laptop, he could have searched for similar patterns. If an Aalana made a pattern a potential mate couldn't recognize, they would feel pleased to have made something original and different. He could only hope Serjeh wouldn't be disappointed or offended.

"It is beautiful. Very pleasing."

"You have no idea what it is."

Een risked a side glance over, but Serjeh was still smiling, perhaps trying not to laugh, and his anxious thoughts calmed. "I do not know. But beautiful, still."

"It's kind of out there, I know." Serjeh got on his knees to face Een and twined their hands together.

"But it's something that you've said that really resonates."

"Yes?"

"Yes. Something that I want every morning, every day that reminds me that you're with me. That we're together." Serjeh cleared his throat and sang the top notes of the Aalana words before repeating the human ones. "My breath greets yours."

A surprised note escaped Een. Now he saw it. The pattern couldn't be clearer. He threw his arms around Serjeh's neck, his lim stroking wherever they could reach. "It is more. Perfect. Beautiful. You are beautiful."

Serjeh held him tight, his breaths shivering. The moisture on Een's shoulder indicated there were tears, but this was not as distressing as it would have been. Tears were for strong emotion, not just for pain and sorrow.

"I was so alone." Serjeh's voice cracked and broke, but he continued. "I never thought... And now you're here and you want to *stay* with me. *Be* with me."

"Always," Een murmured into Serjeh's hair.

"Always," Serjeh whispered.

A black vehicle pulled up beside Serjeh's and Marina stuck her head out of the window. "Hey. Get a room, you two."

"Ha! This is private property, Agent Sanders." The words sounded challenging, but Serjeh still laughed.

"Knock it off." She huffed and came to sit on the top step of the porch with her briefcase beside her. "And you may as well start calling me Marina, since I've been officially assigned as your OAA liaison."

Serjeh scowled at her, but Een didn't think it was

an actual threat display. "The devil you know, I guess. Do you always just barge in like this?"

"Normally, I'd call and set up a meeting." She scowled back. "But *someone* hasn't been answering his phone."

"Oh. Sorry." Serjeh cleared his throat. "I turned it off so Een could rest. Is this an official thing? Should I go get dressed?"

She waved a hand at them. "No. don't bother. It's only semiofficial. I came to drop some things off." Out of the briefcase, she pulled a container the size of her head, a smaller container, and something that looked to Een like one of those *forms* that had irritated Serjeh so much. Before she could reveal the nature of these items, though, she caught sight of the stones. "That's pretty. What are those all about?"

"It's a *munalid*." Serjeh's spine straightened as he said it. "We've been making things official in Aalana."

She stared for a moment, then shook her head. "I feel like we're in new territory with you two all the time. If you want to make it human official...well, that's above my paygrade, but I'll check to see if there's an official policy yet."

"We can wait." Serjeh's smile flashed most of his teeth. "Een still has to meet my parents."

Her snort might have been a laugh. Perhaps. She handed the smaller container to Een. "Setting that aside for the moment, Een, that's a phone. Like Serge's. You need to have your own and the OAA provides. You don't ever have to use it if you don't want to, but it's good to have if you're ever separated from Serge or if we can't reach him for some reason."

"A..." He didn't think he could say the human word

for communication yet. He hadn't practiced it. "A speaking device. Good. Thank you."

"You're welcome." Marina pushed the larger box between them. "This one's more important. The team up at Pitt, medical, biology and biochem, worked twenty-four-hour shifts since you last saw them to get this to you."

Serjeh opened the lid carefully as if he were afraid something might leap out. Inside were two sealed glass bottles containing liquid—one blue, the other red. "Um. Thanks? What is it?"

Marina sighed. "Why are the good-looking ones always dense? Those are chemical equivalents of the gametes from Een's mates. It's in an oil, so I don't think I have to tell you what to do to prevent life-threatening *lim* blockages from developing again."

Face bright red, Serjeh closed the box just as carefully. "Okay. Good. We have to think of something to thank them."

"You can help Een answer their hundred thousand questions about the Aalana. I think that would be birthdays and Christmas all rolled into one for them." Finally, Marina held out the paper. "*This* is a list of possible contractors for the items we discussed. I know you can do it yourself, Mr. Mountain Man, but a team of people would be faster so you and Een can just enjoy the baby when they come."

Serjeh took the list reluctantly. "I do have internet up here, you know. To look up contractors."

"Sure, but you've shown you're not good at contacting people. I've talked to these firms about expanding the porch, getting more windows installed and placing some skylights. You just need to make appointments. That's all. They'll send me the estimates."

"The agency's pretty full service, then?" Serjeh stared at the paper, then at Marina, as if no one had ever offered him assistance before.

"My job's to make sure Een is safe and happy." She snapped her briefcase closed and got up. "If that means finding ways to work with, around or through your neuroses, that's what I'll do."

"Hey!" Serjeh called after her. "I'm not neurotic!"

"So neurotic. But you'll do." Marina waved without turning around. "Go back to canoodling."

Serjeh's jaw dropped open in that way it did when he lost words, so Een sang after her, "Thank you!"

After Marina had driven away, he turned to Serjeh. "What is *canoodling*?"

––––––

THEY LEFT the stones where they were. Een implied the final partner to answer the *munalid* got the last word. Eventually, they'd have to pick up the impromptu art display so the contractors could work on the porch and not slide around on little round rocks. But not now. Instead, Serge had his breakfast while calling the suggested contractors, then got his shower and slid into a fleece robe.

He followed Een's voice to find him, not shockingly, singing to Naim in the front room. The theory seemed to be the same as it was for human babies—the little ones could hear music in the womb, er, pod, so parents sang and played songs close to the tank. He hummed along—he knew the tune even if he hadn't learned all the Aalana words—and when the song ended, he pulled Een into his arms.

"You know, we should probably test those oils to be sure the scientists got it right."

"Yes." Een nodded seriously, his *lim* wandering toward Serge. "Testing is important."

He leaned in to whisper in Een's ear. "Not in front of Naim, though."

Een trilled a laugh and ran a finger over the V where Serge's collarbones met. "Sleeping platform is softer."

"It is." Serge checked the front door, readjusted Naim's sunlamp, tucked the box with the oils under his arm, and took Een by the hands, backing toward the hallway and the bedrooms as Een followed with shining eyes.

Once they reached Serge's room, Een plucked at the robe, singing in his saddest minor chord, "Coverings."

"You're allowed to take them off me." Serge ran a teasing hand over the erratically waving *lim*. Then hastily amended his statement. "I mean, not whenever you feel like it. But when we're, ah, mating."

Een's little trill was more purr than laugh as he tugged the tie free on the bathrobe. The pads of his fingers, more deeply striated than a human's, tugged deliciously at Serge's carpet of chest fur. The robe puddled to the floor and Serge stepped closer, shivering with delight at the brush of Een's *faiina* on naked skin.

He stilled when Een's hand closed around his erection. "Hmm. While that's wonderful, maybe we should take out time today."

"But this pleases?" Een clicked his tongue in confusion as Serge gently removed his hand.

"It does. It really does. But I don't want to rush." Serge searched for a different way to put it when Een still cocked his head to the side. "This can be last. Lots of things are pleasing."

"You wish foreplay." Een tugged him toward the bed with a little smile.

Serge snorted a laugh. "Yeah. That. It's hard to keep up with the words you've learned sometimes."

"Human mating. Much putting things into other things."

"Sometimes, yeah." Serge still chuckled as he put the box on the bedside table and stretched out next to Een. "But not always."

Een hummed and nuzzled at his throat. "This pleases?"

"Oh, yeah. Most places you touch are going to be." Serge squirmed away when a lim went in his ear. "Okay. Maybe not that."

"Sorry." Another word Een had gotten a good handle on recently. "My *lim*... They do not listen with you."

While a miniature sun formed in Serge's chest at the realization that Een lost control around him, another *lim* was trying for an ear dive. He squirmed up toward the headboard a little, just to get his ears out of reach. With that accomplished, Een concentrated on his chest and shoulders, the velvet softness of the *lim* making Serge arch and moan.

"Your *lim* might have bad aim, but they feel so *good*."

Serge buried both hands in those sensitive waving

tubes, pleased when Een trill-purred and squirmed on top of him. More than pleased. Between Een's hands and his *lim*, he seemed to stroke everywhere at once and those dragon feather-scales pressing down on Serge's cock made it impossible to keep his hips still.

He tried his best to keep up, stroking and petting the *lim*. They swelled in his hands as Een matched his squirming arousal, but not like the painful engorgement when Een was dying. When he ran a finger just inside the opening of one, Een gave a gasping chirrup and squirmed harder.

Yes on the lim rimming, then.

Trying it with his tongue had mixed results. Een enjoyed it enormously, but Serge ended up getting thwapped in the face with excited appendages with increasing speed and had to stop. Then as he stroked his hands down Een's throat, he came to an abrupt halt when Een stilled.

"Hey. You okay?"

Carefully, Een removed Serge's hands. "Not there. Too much stoma."

Serge jerked his hands away in horror. He'd been cutting off the majority of Een's air since he breathed more through his stomata than his mouth or nose. "Oh, crap. Sorry. Sorry. Anywhere else?"

Een shook his head vigorously, smacking Serge in the face again with flying *lim*.

"Oof. Pff. Okay, good." Laughing, Serge put an arm up to defend his face. "I should write an article. *All the Things You Should Ask Your Offworld Lover.*"

Missteps out of the way for now, they did better finding a rhythm of hips and hands that delighted them both. Heat began to roll off Een, his coloring brightening to amethyst.

"Are you close?" Serge whispered in his ear as he rolled them over so he straddled Een.

"Close. Yes." Een sang, his hands stroking desperately over Serge's cock and balls.

Serge blew out a breath and squeezed his eyes shut, trying to hang on as Een's fingers closed harder around him. "Mother of... Me too. Chest? For oils?"

"Chest... Shoulders... Face..." Een panted out. "I do not care."

Hands shaking, Serge put the box on the bed between them and the wall. If he fumbled a bottle, he didn't want it dropping to the floor and breaking. The university could make more, sure, but these oils still felt too precious, the magic elixir that would keep Een healthy. *And with me.* The thought was both fierce and a little selfish, but they did have a child to think of now, too. *For both of us, then. For our family.*

The bottles had labels simply marked with *1* on the red and *2* on the blue, clear even to a non-scientist that these referred to the order of application. He uncapped the red bottle, which had a glass applicator reminiscent of a perfume bottle. *Very thoughtful.*

Een had stilled, watching every movement. The moment Serge applied a thin line of red oil, Een threw his head back against the pillows, his *lim* straining forward as he crooned.

"That's it. You're so beautiful," Serge whispered in response as he uncapped the blue bottle and added the second line.

He just had time to replace the precious oils and close the box before Een's fist closed around his cock again in hard, sure strokes. Serge cried out and fell forward with his hands on either side of Een's head, rubbing his cheek against the straining lim.

"You can do it, Een. Oh God, I'm so close. Come on, love."

Unlike the first time when Een was in such terrible pain, this time his climax was fluid and glorious. He arched his back, lifting Serge with him, and sang a triumphant five-chord sequence again and again. The white ropes of his pollen splashed Serge even as his own orgasm roared over him. He bucked and cried out in time to Een's music, the fountains of their come meeting between them and drawing wavering patterns on their bodies.

"Beautiful," Serge whispered when he found words again and he collapsed onto his side next to Een.

Humming softly now, Een gathered him close, his spent *lim* falling around his head as if they'd fallen asleep without him. "The oils are good."

"We'll have to tell them." Serge put an arm over Een's chest, not concerned about the mess and not wanting to leave Een's warmth yet. "I hope they don't want us to keep, I dunno, journals about it."

"Data is not easy." Een stroked up and down Serge's back. "How long. How much. We have no measuring."

Serge snorted on a laugh. "I see. Now you've got jokes. I'm *not* talking to them about getting measuring devices for all this. And they don't get to know details. Just that it worked really well."

"I am...not anxious now? After anxious?" Een raised his head to look at Serge. "Is there a word?"

"Relieved. Yeah, me too. So relieved that you'll be

okay now." Serge kissed his cheek. "Een? I was thinking, with the baby coming, and the guest room really should be the nursery..."

"You wish to share sleeping rooms?"

"I do. Would you like that?"

Een hugged him tighter. "I do like this. Sleeping only me is...strange. Not right."

"Good." Serge sighed and snuggled closer. "Good. I'll start clearing stuff out tomorrow. Do baby Aalana need cribs?"

"I do not know this word."

Serge smiled against the soft *faiina* of Een's chest. "Time to introduce you to the wonderful world of human baby furniture. You'll have research to keep you busy for weeks."

EPILOGUE_

Serge was stenciling a chair rail of ferns around the guest room, which would soon become the baby's room, with the door closed. Marina Saunders, he'd stopped tormenting her with the wrong name, was meeting with Een in private for their monthly check-in. Procedure. Serge understood that now. There couldn't be any question of him constraining Een or influencing his answers in any way. For his part, Een enjoyed the visits, eager for the chance to practice his swiftly improving language skills. He even played host since he'd learned to make coffee and he insisted Serge always have *small cakes* on hand for human visitors.

The sudden wail from the front room made him drop the paintbrush on his foot and nearly stopped his heart. He ripped open the door and raced to the front of the house, nearly taking himself out on the corner at the end of the hall while Een called out in full operatic voice, "Serjeh! Serjeh!"

"What's wrong? What?" Serge pulled Een into his

arms, glaring accusingly at Marina. Damn her, she just smiled at him. "Een! What's happened?"

Een pointed to Naim's nursery tank, singing rapid-fire Aalana words.

"Whoa, slow down." Serge stroked the *faiina* of Een's back, surprised that they were soft and settled. If Een was so upset, then why...? Oh. *Oh.* "Naim's hatching? Or bursting? Or whatever it is?"

He leaned close to the tank in time to see a long crack in the pod widen. A tiny hand forced its way out, a perfect little shoulder shoving against the pod to open it farther. Een clung to him, shivering, his silver eyes wide. The flow of words settled to a lovely crooning, perhaps a song of welcome or encouragement.

"Hey." Serge turned Een to get his full attention. "What do we do? Do we help?"

With an alarmed trill, Een took both of Serge's hands. "No. She must...come out. Without us. It is important. When she is out, we can lift her. Then she can be in air. With us. Without the...struggle, her stomas do not open. Not be ready for air."

"She? You're sure now?"

"Yes. The fingers, the *lim* are different." Een nodded to the tank where a beautiful round head with tiny vermicelli-sized *lim* waved and twitched. "She. Naim. Our Naim."

Serge hugged him tight, watching her emergence from the pod in rapt fascination though his sight kept blurring with tears.

"Congratulations, you two," Marina said softly, as if afraid to disturb the moment.

"Thank you," Een sang as the first leg kicked free of

the cracked pod. When Naim shoved herself out, kicking the pod away from her, he lifted the lid from the tank. "Serjeh, now. Together."

Serge reached a hand in at the same time Een did, and together they lifted the tiny, perfect Aalana child from the water, her body barely big enough to cover their joined palms. She wriggled and kicked, opening her silver eyes to stare up at them and let out a clear, perfectly pitched triad cry. With her first sounds, Een was no longer the only Aalana voice on the planet, and with the government helping to gather information and the technical expertise from other resident aliens, perhaps more would join them some day.

Someday, too, the faceless enemy that had chased the Aalana across the stars might arrive, but the refugees had come to the right planet, one with experience in all things martial and destructive. Hell, humans had engaged each other in warfare throughout their entire history, almost as if they'd been practicing for this. Together, they would be prepared.

Naim kicked the heel of Serge's thumb and cried out again, yanking him back from his wandering thoughts.

"Welcome, little one. Our breath greets yours," Een sang softly. "We are your parents, Een and Serjeh."

She caught hold of Serge's thumb and clung on hard, her strength astounding. Serge leaned in to kiss her button nose and whisper, "Welcome." In the circle of Een's embrace, in the earnest regard of those newborn silver eyes, the universe became whole again.

GLOSSARY_

Aalana – a photophagic spacefaring people who communicate in harmonies and sung notes. Triad mating groups are necessary for reproduction: male, female and *nen*. Digestive and circulatory structures have more in common with Earth plants than animals.

Faiina – an Aalana's dermal covering consisting of triangular overlapping pieces. Under normal circumstances, these are soft, not unlike feathers, but when an Aalana feels threatened or is startled, the *faiina* swiftly fill with rah to form sharp, defensive spikes.

Lim – the tentacle-like tubular structures atop an Aalana's head. Unlike hair, these are tactile, mobile, serve as particulate filters for a more sensitive method of smell than humans, and can shoot either *melai* when threatened or also, in males during reproduction, pollen.

Melai – a mild neurotoxin propelled from an Aalana's *lim* to immobilize an attacker. Only used in extreme circumstances.

Munalid – an Aalana courtship ritual involving the creation of patterns from small items to indicate mating intentions.

Nen – the Aalana third gender. Nen provide spores during mating and are the necessary catalyst for conception of young.

Rah – an Aalana's circulatory fluid, thicker and stickier than blood.

Thank you for purchasing ***Eating Stars***. Oh, and if Angel had you laughing and smiling with her unique perspective on the human—*and alien*—experience, you should check out her *Offbeat Crimes* series. Who doesn't love a paranormal misfits squad? Or take a dive into her *Brimstone* series where drag queen AIs placate a thieving, and unfortunately, exiled demon from Earth.

Please consider leaving a review where you purchased this ebook or on Goodreads. Reviews and word-of-mouth recommendations are vital to independent publishers.

Want to hear the latest news about Angel and other Mischiefer releases and titles? Visit our website: http://www.mischiefcornerbooks.com and join our newsletter.

As always, enjoy reading!
Mischief Corner Books

http://www.mischiefcornerbooks.com

Brandywine
Investigations
OPEN for Business
Angel Martinez

While Angel Martinez is the erotic fiction pen name of a writer of several genres, she writes both kinds of gay romance – Science Fiction and Fantasy. Currently living part time in the hectic sprawl of northern Delaware, (and full time inside the author's head) Angel has one husband, one son, two cats, a changing variety of other furred and scaled companions, a love of all things beautiful and a terrible addiction to the consumption of both knowledge and chocolate.

For more information on Angel's work, please visit:

Official Website:
http://angelmartinezauthor.weebly.com/

Email:
angelmartinezauthor@gmail.com

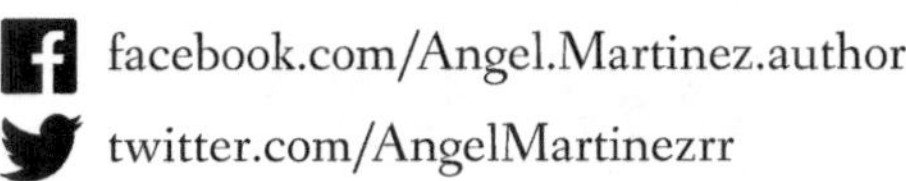
facebook.com/Angel.Martinez.author
twitter.com/AngelMartinezrr

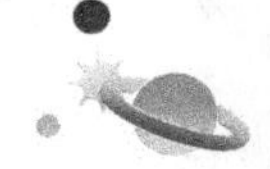

Safety Protocols for Human Holidays

Yule Planet

The Solstice Pudding

BRANDYWINE INVESTIGATIONS

Brandywine Investigations: Open for Business (Omnibus)

Brandywine Investigations: Family Matters (Omnibus)

BRIMSTONE

Potato Surprise #1

Hell for the Company #2

Fear of Frogs #3

Shax's War #4

Beside a Black Tarn #5

The Hunt for Red Fluffy #6

A Fine Mess #7 (Summer 2020)

The Brimstone Journals: Collection One

The Brimstone Journals: Collection Two

The Brimstone Journals: Collection Three

THE ENDANGERED FAE SERIES

Finn

Diego

Semper Fae

No Fae is an Island

ESTO UNIVERSE

Vassily the Beautiful

Prisoner 374215

A Matter of Faces

Gravitational Attraction

SubZero (Summer 2020)

LIJUN Trilogy (with Freddy Mackay)

Fireworks & Stolen Kisses

Trysts & Burning Embers

Detonations & Devotion (TBD)

**INTERPLANETARY MULTISPECIES
PACT (IMP)**

A Christmas Cactus for the General

A Message from the Home Office (Summer 2020)

THE WEB OF ARCANA

The Mage on the Hill

OFFBEAT CRIMES

Lime Gelatin and Other Monsters

Pill Bugs of Time

Skim Blood & Savage Verse

Feral Dust Bunnies

Jackalopes & Woofen-Poofs

All the World's an Undead Stage

SINGLE TITLES

The Color of His Crest

Hearts & Flowers: A Tale of Hay Fever and Bad Decor

Restoration

The Line

AURA UNIVERSE (with Bellora Quinn)

Quinn's Gambit

Flax's Pursuit

Kellen's Awakening